THE *Wife* MAKER

USA Today Bestselling Author
KAREY WHITE

Orange Door Press

ISBN: 978-1-941898-07-9

Published by Orange Door Press

For Renae

*The match maker who
made my husband
a wife maker*

Thank you!

I love you.

Chapter 1

Angus

I banged on the wall, hoping the guy next door would turn down his offensive music. Most of the time I could just tune it out, but right now it felt like a prize fighter clobbering his way through my skull.

What had just happened? I tried to replay the last twenty minutes, but my mind couldn't make sense of it. I hadn't expected to see Charles at my front door. I hadn't seen her since her birthday. What a mistake that had been. A piece of advice—all those Hallmark movies my mom watches are a bunch of garbage. They'd have you believe that all it takes for the best friend to win the leading lady's heart is a courageous declaration and a romantic kiss.

Not true. It had taken me years to overcome my fear of telling Charlotte how I feel. And what had been the reward for that great act of courage? A humiliating rejection and—you guessed it—no more best friend. Definitely not the stuff chick flicks are made of.

If Charlotte knocking on my door had been a surprise, the reason she was there was such a shock it was hard to process. Had she really come to tell me she loved me? I'd been waiting for her to say those words for most of my adult life. If she had said them two months earlier, life would have been perfect—Alameda residency, Charles, and me. We'd probably be engaged already. When you know someone so well, have been through all the good and bad of the past fifteen years, and have been in love with her for about half of that, it's not really rushing into anything.

Nice of Charles to decide she loves me after I'm committed to a program that will put me two-thousand miles away from San Francisco.

There was no way out now. I had already given up my residency spot at Alameda County Medical Center. I couldn't back out of Kansas City unless I wanted my entire career left in ruins. Chuck and I had always had bad timing, but she'd really stepped up her game this time.

The guy on the other side of the wall banged back so hard I was surprised his fist didn't appear through the wall. He said a few words I was glad Chuck wasn't still around to hear, then he cranked the volume up even higher. Nice. Thanks for nothing. My thin-walled apartment was one thing I wouldn't miss when I moved to Kansas City. Hopefully my new apartment would have quiet neighbors. Maybe a bookworm or a mathematician. Anything but the gangsta rap and metal-crushing action movies that dominated this guy's life.

I needed to get out of this apartment. I needed to think. I grabbed my keys and headed for the car.

I didn't have a destination in mind when I started driving. I just turned off the radio and drove, letting my thoughts keep me company.

I hadn't wanted to see Chuck standing outside my door. I didn't even know she was back from Scotland. If she hadn't seen me through the glass, I'm not sure I'd have let her in. I was trying to get her out of my system, and standing there, a nervous smile on her face, she'd looked good. Too good.

Chuck is one of those girls that doesn't know how gorgeous she is. She looks like a supermodel, but better, because she never looks like she's trying too hard. She has these incredible eyes that look brown until you get closer, and then you get lost in the green and gold flecks. And her eyes can speak. I can always tell how she's feeling by looking in her eyes. I love how they shine when she's excited or twinkle when she finds something funny. Too many times over the last few years, they've been sad. For a long time I thought I could be the one to put the light back in them, but she's never given me the chance.

Until now. When it's too late.

Oh, Charles. Why did you have to throw me such a curveball? I thought I'd stepped off the Charlotte roller coaster. Why did you have to drag me back on?

I pulled up to the curb and put the car in park. I was a little stunned to discover I was sitting in front of Will's house. I guess I shouldn't have been too surprised. Will has always been the guy I go to when a girl has my mind in a muddle.

Will was mowing his lawn, mouthing the words to whatever song was playing through his earbuds. I turned off the car and watched a boy down the block as he practiced flipping his skateboard. He'd mastered the skateboard part. It twisted through the air and landed on its wheels every time. The part he struggled with was landing on top of the board. He hit the side twice and then nearly face planted when he hit the front of the board. I winced and wished he was wearing a helmet.

Suddenly the passenger door flew open, startling me.

"Hey, man. What's up?" Will leaned down to look at me inside the car.

"Not much. Just out for a drive to clear my head, and I ended up here."

"It's about time. You've been AWOL for weeks." My face must have given away my mood because his tone changed. "Hey, you okay?"

I didn't answer, just shrugged.

Will slapped the roof of the car. "You want to spill it here or go somewhere?"

I sighed. It was good to have a friend who knew when something was up. "Is Gina home?"

"Yeah."

"You good if we go for a drive?"

"Sure. Just let me tell her I'm leaving." Will pushed the lawn mower up by the porch and hollered through the front door. "Hey babe, I'm going for a drive with Angus."

Gina followed Will to the car, smiling. Will scored big time when he met her. I'd have been resentful that it had all come so easily to Will, but I loved him too much to hate him for his good fortune.

"Hi, Angus."

My smile must have been unsuccessful because Gina's smile quickly changed to an expression of concern. "Is something wrong?"

"Not really. Just a lot going on right now. Is it okay if I borrow your husband for a while?"

"Of course."

"Need anything while we're out?" Will asked.

"I don't think so." She turned back to me. "Are you busy later? You could eat with us when you come back."

"I wish I could, but I've got to be at the hospital."

"Too bad. Maybe another time," Gina said.

"Yeah. Sounds good."

We didn't have anywhere to go and I only had an hour before I would need to head back, so I pulled into the parking lot of a Target and parked in a nearly empty corner. Now that I was here with Will, I wasn't even sure what to tell him. Charlotte was his twin sister, after all.

"Where ya been?" Will asked. "I've been trying to reach you for weeks."

I looked out the windshield, my hands resting on the bottom of the steering wheel. "I've been figuring out a few things."

"Did you break up with Charlotte's friend?"

"Yeah. It sucked. She was pretty upset. She cried and cried."

"That's rough."

"I should never have let Chuck set us up in the first place. It was a mistake."

"Is that why you disappeared, or is something else going on?"

I squared my shoulders. "I'm leaving."

"What are you talking about?" Will turned in his seat to face me, but I kept my eyes fixed on the smiley faced star of the Carl's Jr. logo across the street.

"I'm moving to Kansas City."

"Kansas City? What's in Kansas City?"

"Dr. Fickland heard about a hip fellowship there. I'm

taking it."

"What about Alameda? And your residency?"

"I'll be doing the fellowship and my residency simultaneously."

"I didn't know you could leave. I thought you'd be here at least until you finished."

"It doesn't happen often, and if Fickland wasn't behind it, it wouldn't work. But it's a great opportunity. I'm lucky I was chosen."

Will sunk back in his seat and we both stared at a Little League team piling out of two minivans, laughing and shoving their way into the restaurant. "Whoa. I can't believe you're moving." Will sighed. "I guess that makes Charlotte a no-go, right?"

"What do you mean?"

Will folded his arms. "You said a while back . . . I thought you were going to ask her out."

"That was before she took off to visit Braveheart."

"Dude, you're sounding a little bitter."

"Maybe I feel a little bitter. It'll be good to get away from that whole mess."

"I'm not sure where Charlotte's head is when it comes to you, but I think you've got the wrong idea about the guy from Scotland. They're just friends. Chuck even set him up with a girl she met while she was there."

I shook my head. "Let's hope he fares better from her matchmaking efforts than I did. Or Aleena. Maybe Chuck should stick to drawing roller coasters."

Will didn't respond and a little guilt tugged at my conscience. Will was Charlotte's brother before he was my friend. I needed to be careful not to push his loyalty too far.

Will shook his head. "Kansas City. Charles will be shocked."

"She already knows." Will looked surprised. "She came by this afternoon."

"She did? How did she take it?"

I shrugged.

Will's eyes searched my face. "Why did she stop by?"

"Aleena told her we broke up and that I was moving. She came to see if it was true."

"I'll bet she wasn't happy that she had to find out from someone else. Did she read you the riot act?"

I didn't answer. I leaned my head back on the headrest and closed my eyes.

"Angus? What happened today?"

I didn't answer immediately. Will waited, and I could feel his eyes boring into me.

"She came to tell me she loves me."

"Dude. You're kidding. That's great. Maybe the two of you can stop dancing around each other like blind fools."

"Don't get too excited, Will. Nothing's happening."

"Why not? I thought this was what you wanted."

"It was."

"Then what's the problem?"

"I'm leaving. I'll be gone for four years. Four years. Do you know how long that is?" I sighed. "It just wasn't meant to be."

"Oh, come on. When did you become such a pessimist?"

"I'm serious, man. If we ever had a chance, it's gone now. I was the patient, lovesick puppy for long enough. Now I'm moving to Kansas City and starting over." I lowered my voice. "I tried. And I'm not interested in being Chuck's consolation prize."

"What do you mean you tried? It sounds like she was the one who finally tried." There was an edge in Will's voice and

I could tell his stick-up-for-my-sister hackles were appearing.

"She knew how I felt before she went chasing halfway around the world after some guy she barely knew. That told me everything I needed to know."

"Are you sure she knew how you felt?"

I gave a short nod. "I told her. On your birthday."

Will thought for a second and then a look of understanding passed over his face. "Is that why she was so flustered that day? And why you left early? Man, what did you say?"

"I kissed her. I told her how I felt." Will looked like he might choke. "And then she left the country."

Will whistled. "That's rough."

"I'm done, man. This is a great chance for me to further my career, and I've got to get out of this rut." I shook my head. "I've been waiting for way too long. Every time she had her heart broken, I was there. It was me she came to when she found out people were calling her the husband maker. I wanted to be the one to fix things for her, but she never let me."

Even as I said it, I felt horrible. I'd been loyal to Charles for so long that even saying this to Will made me feel uncomfortable.

"But she loves you."

"Too bad she didn't realize that before I changed the whole course of my life."

I was proud of myself for sounding so self-assured, so certain that I knew what I was doing. I knew if I said it often enough, I could get past my feelings for Charlotte. Moving away was the best thing I could do. I needed a clean break. Maybe there was a reason Charles and I had always had bad timing. This would give us both a chance to clear our heads and move on with our lives.

Chapter 2

Charlotte

"*L*et's get double use out of these drawings and put them on both the postcards and the mugs." I had just presented a proposal for the Sunset Safari Wild Animal Park to Bryce Cardell. He'd liked the proposal, but I could tell by his questions that he was worried about the cost. "That would save you some money."

Bryce moved a few of the sketches to the side. "I like all of this, but we're on a tight budget and our top priority is the map of the park."

"I understand. But if we multi-purpose some of these, it'll save you money and you'll have a better selection in the gift shop. You might also consider printing the map in two sizes— the smaller one to give visitors as they come through the park and a larger, poster-sized one to sell in the gift shop."

"Ah, that's a great idea."

Mr. Cardell chose the rough sketches he wanted me to create, signed a contract, and I walked him to the elevator.

"Sunset Safari Park is going with us." I paused at the door of Jayne's office on my way back to gather my things in the conference room.

"That's good news." Jayne took a deep breath. "Charlotte, can you come in here for a minute? And close the door."

Was this serious? I couldn't remember Jayne ever asking me to close the door. She'd even told me about Kyle's engagement with the door open.

"Congratulations on the new account. Of course he liked your proposal. I did a smart thing when I put you over souvenirs."

I smiled. I had been creating promotional tourism materials and souvenirs for more than four years now, and I loved it. I got paid to draw and color. I probably had the best job in the world. "We trimmed it back a bit. He was worried about money, so we eliminated a few things, but he seems happy."

"We like happy clients." Jayne clasped her hands and rested her chin on her knuckles. "Charlotte, is everything okay?"

"Sure. This just closed and I have a meeting next Monday with Rent and Ride, that bicycle company. They have over twenty locations, so that might be a good account."

"I'm not talking about work."

"Oh." I sat back in my chair. I hadn't told anyone about what was happening—or not happening—in my life. Of course there was Angus, but he hadn't come after me and probably wouldn't, which meant there wasn't much to tell. To be honest, I was sick of talking about dating and romance and love. I was tired of talking about guys period.

"Maybe I'm imagining things, but you haven't seemed quite yourself since you got back from Scotland."

So much for trying to put up a good front. "Everything is

fine."

"You had a good time?"

"It was the best trip of my life."

"Are you sad to be back? Are you missing your Scotsman?"

If only it were that simple. "The first few days I was pretty jetlagged, but I'm good now." I had been home for nearly three weeks, so the jetlag was long gone. "I loved Scotland and Flynn is great, but I'm not sad to be back and he's not my Scotsman."

"You're not still sad about Kyle, are you?"

"No. Not at all. I'm really okay. I'm sorry if I've worried you."

Jayne shook her head and waved me off. "Oh please. Don't be sorry about me. I just want to be sure you're all right."

"I'm great. Really. I'd better get that proposal out of the conference room before Keith spills his lunch on it." I walked to the door.

Jayne smiled. "Good job on Safari."

"Thanks." I paused. "And thanks for checking on me."

I'd just lied to my boss and friend. Things weren't good at all. Aleena still wouldn't take my calls. And Angus wanted nothing to do with me. This had happened in the past with guys I'd dated, but this was different. This was Angus. He was the one who had helped me get over those other guys. Who was going to help me get over Angus?

I felt sick. I couldn't even imagine going on without him. He had been there for almost every important event in my life. How could he not be there anymore?

It still surprised me how sure I was about my feelings for Angus. It's a little like when I saw *The Sixth Sense*. I had been completely blown away at the end when I learned that Bruce Willis's character had been dead the whole movie. And then it was like, "Duh! Of course. It all makes sense now. Why didn't I figure that out earlier?"

After Angus kissed me, I knew. I just had to be willing to admit it. And once I admitted it, I had to figure out what to do about it. If I'd minded my own business, he and Aleena wouldn't have been dating and everything would have been different. Instead of filling me with guilt and confusion, that kiss would have been the best birthday present of my life. But I had run away and left Angus standing there. Now he was leaving me and I didn't know how to make him stay.

My plan had been to tell Angus how I felt, kiss him senseless, and then plan our future together. Simplistic, I know, but I really thought it would be as easy as that. Now I was facing four years of a long-distance relationship and that was only if I somehow convinced Angus that we should actually be *in* a relationship. At this point, he seemed pretty set on hating me.

But no matter how long it took me to convince Angus that he shouldn't give up on us, I needed to snap out of my funk. No way did I want to be a glum Gladys for the next four years, sucking the fun and energy out of the room whenever I was there. If I was going to patiently wait out the next four years, I needed to do it cheerfully.

It was hard to put my despondent mood behind me when I knew I had hurt my two best friends. Mending things with Angus was tricky because I wanted to be more than friends. Since I had no idea how I was going to accomplish that, I decided to focus my energy on making peace with Aleena. I'd texted her at least a dozen times in the last three weeks, but she hadn't responded. I had called her cell phone twice, but she hadn't picked up. I decided I'd have to be brave and risk seeing Aleena's father. The last time I'd spoken to him, he had scolded me like I was a little child. I knew he usually took Thursdays off, so when Thursday rolled around, I went to their restaurant for lunch.

I was disappointed to see a girl I didn't know working the front of the restaurant. I had hoped it would be Aleena there.

"How many in your party?" she asked.

"Just me."

"Right this way."

I followed the girl to a small table by the window. I opened the menu even though I didn't need it.

"Charlotte. I thought that was you." John, a waiter I'd met several times, smiled down at me.

"Hi, John."

"What can I get for you?"

"I'd like the cashew chicken."

John wrote on his pad. "Is Aleena eating with you?"

I felt a surge of relief that my betrayal of Aleena wasn't common knowledge among the staff. "Is she working?"

"Yeah. She's back in the office. I'll tell her you're here."

Too bad John was already married when he started working in the Li's restaurant. He had a nice smile that would look good next to Aleena's. I shook my head. I needed to stop worrying about my friend's love life. Wasn't that why I was in this mess in the first place?

I wiped my hands on my skirt. What a pathetic position I'd put myself in. I loved Aleena. We'd been friends for years, but here I sat about to hyperventilate, I was so nervous to face her.

Several minutes passed. I was about to step back to the office when I saw her. She stopped at the hostess stand and said something to the girl working there. I smiled and waved when her eyes skimmed the room, but if she saw me, she pretended not to. A moment later, she walked out the front door. I should have followed her, but instead I sat there stunned as I watched her cross the street and head down the opposite sidewalk.

A few minutes later John brought me a plate of cashew chicken. "Did you talk to Aleena before she left?"

I swallowed hard. "No. She must have been in a hurry."

"Really? She said she had to run an errand, but I thought she'd stop and say hi first."

"It's no problem. I'll catch up with her another time."

"Enjoy your meal."

I tried to eat. I normally love the cashew chicken, but today I could barely choke down a few bites, and what I did eat, I didn't taste. Would I ever have a chance to explain myself to Aleena?

I motioned for John. "Would you mind packing this up to go? I've got to get back to the office."

"No problem."

"And would you ask Aleena to call me when she has a minute?"

"Sure thing."

Chapter 3

Charlotte

uly 9.

Me: Hey Angus.

It took nine minutes before my phone beeped with his response.

Angus: Hi.

Me: How's it going?

Fourteen minutes later.

Angus: Not too bad.

Me: That's good. Have you seen Will's new deck?

Yes, I was grasping at straws, but what could I do? Angus was leaving next month and I wanted to have some kind of contact with him. How could I get him to change his mind about loving me if I completely disappeared from his life?

Eleven minutes later.

Angus: I didn't know he was doing a new deck.

Me: They decided it would be their summer project. It looks great. He's even building a pergola.

Nine minutes later.

Angus: Nice.

Me: Who knew home ownership would make Will such a handyman?

Sixteen minutes later.

Angus: I'll have to stop by sometime and check it out.

Me: Yeah. Well, I guess I'll see ya later.

I checked my phone for the next hour, but Angus never responded.

July 17

Me: Did you see the Giants game last night?

Angus: I haven't had time this summer.

Me: Oh, too bad. Last night went into extra innings. The Giants won 8-7 in twelve innings.

Twenty-two minutes later. But who's counting?

Angus: Sounds exciting.

Me: I only started watching it in the eighth inning, but the finish was great.

Seventeen minutes later.

Angus: When did you start caring about baseball?

Me: I usually don't, but Mia and Graham were watching it and I kinda got hooked at the end.

Twenty-six minutes later.

Angus: I'll bet your dad enjoyed it.

Me: He missed it. They went out to dinner with the Paulson's and got home as it was ending. Dad was seriously bummed.

Twelve minutes later.

Angus: That's too bad.

Me: Yeah. Of course he forgot to record it. Can you believe that? Best game of the year and all he gets are ESPN highlights.

July 23

Me: When do you leave for Kansas City?

Nineteen minutes later.

Angus: August 11

Me: Oh, that's so soon.

TWO MINUTES LATER! I was thrilled with the response time.

Angus: I'm excited to get on my way.

Oh. Not so thrilling after all.

Me: Don't forget we need to go out to dinner.

Twenty minutes later.

Angus: Right.

I threw my phone onto the other side of the couch and concentrated on a television show about some people who were selling Pez dispensers they'd found in a storage unit. The obnoxious guy, who spit when he talked, kissed his girlfriend when he found out the Mr. Potato Head dispenser he had was worth over two-thousand dollars. I mean a full-on, makeout kiss. If he could have her, why couldn't I have Angus?

July 30

Me: Need any help packing?

Seventeen minutes later.

Angus: No thanks. I've got it under control.

Me: Are you renting a moving truck?

Eleven minutes later.

Angus: No. Storing my things at Dad and Mom's.

Me: I guess you'll have to find a furnished apartment.

Sixteen minutes later.

Me again: Have you already found an apartment?

I was feeling a little pathetic and almost didn't hit the send button.

Five minutes later.

Angus: The supervising doctor gave me some recommendations.

Me: That's good.

Me: Are you sure you want to go? It's not too late to change your mind. ☺

One minute later.

Angus: Actually it is.

Me: I know. I was just kidding.

I've decided helium balloons were created as a sick joke on humanity. If you don't believe me, watch someone try to load a balloon bouquet into the back seat of a Volkswagen bug on a windy, San Francisco day. It's the stuff that belongs in *Dumb and Dumber*. The balloons were like trick candles. As soon as I pushed the last one in, another one would pop back out. I should have bought McKayla a bouquet of flowers to go with the soft, frog-covered blanket instead of a dozen temperamental, floating orbs. Come to think of it, balloons were a pretty lame choice. My newborn nephew wouldn't care one whit about them, and now Connor and McKayla would have to worry about getting them home.

Traffic was heavy, and it took more than an hour to get to the hospital. I maneuvered the balloons into the elevator and punched the button for the fourth floor. The door of Room 433 was slightly ajar. I started to push it open when I heard Angus's voice and froze.

"Thanks for having this little guy before I leave."

"I did it all for you, Angus." McKayla sounded happy.

Angus laughed and I realized it was a sound I hadn't heard for months. It made me sad.

"He's a beauty." His voice changed as he talked to the baby. "But I guess since you're a little man you might not want to be called a beauty, huh?"

"When do you leave?" Connor asked.

"Monday, bright and early."

Monday? Monday wasn't the eleventh. Monday was the sixth. And it was only three days from now. I sagged against the wall. I'd made no progress in my win-Angus-back campaign, and now he was leaving five days earlier than he'd told me.

"I've heard winters can be pretty rough there," Connor said.

"It will be an adjustment, for sure. But getting a chance like this is too big to pass up. I'm lucky Dr. Fickland thought about me."

"You must have impressed him," McKayla said.

I took a deep breath and pushed the door open. I hadn't seen Angus since that awful day at his apartment. He looked good. You'd have thought I'd taken the stairs to the fourth floor as out of breath as I was. It struck me what a strange thing it was that I could spend nineteen years with no noticeable reaction to being around Angus and then suddenly a kiss could make every nerve ending aware of his presence.

"Congratulations!" I said, noticing a manic quality in my voice.

And then those devil balloons started mocking me. First one of the strings caught on the lever door handle, which disrupted the whole bundle of them and then one of them was stuck in the space by the door hinges. I tried to yank them into the room, but the ribbon on the one stuck in the gap snapped and it slowly rose to the ceiling. I felt conspicuous and silly as I wrangled the remaining balloons into a symmetrical bouquet.

"Here. Get these horrible things away from me," I said, handing the balloons off to Connor.

McKayla and Connor were grinning and even Angus looked amused.

"They're just balloons," Connor said.

"No they're not. They're demon balloons and they hate me."

"At least they're adorable," McKayla said.

"Let me see that sweet little guy," I said, stepping closer

to Angus, who was holding him. I leaned over and lifted the blanket farther away from the baby's face. "Oh, you guys, he's so cute." His little cheeks were ruddy and chubby. Dark hair hugged his round head. I touched his cheek with the back of my finger and his lips started moving.

"You want to hold him?" Angus asked.

"Yes, but I don't want to cut your turn short."

"It's okay. I've been holding him for a while." I silently cursed the traffic that had kept me from arriving earlier.

Angus stood and motioned for me to take the rocking chair he'd been sitting in. I glanced around the room and was disappointed to see there were no empty chairs. I wanted him to stay for as long as possible.

"Thanks." I settled into the chair and Angus carefully passed the baby into my arms. The backs of his hands brushed my arms as he pulled them out from under the precious little bundle, and something seized at my heart. Suddenly I felt like crying. No, that's not quite right. I was crying. A tear slipped down my cheek and I shrugged my shoulder up to wipe it away with my shirt. I looked down at my wonderful nephew and another tear fell. And then another.

"Charlotte, are you okay?" McKayla asked quietly.

"I'm fine. He's just so perfect."

"I know."

Connor stood and slid his chair next to mine. "Here, Angus. I promised McKayla I'd go get her chocolate."

"You can't handle the emotion in the room." McKayla laughed and reached her hand toward Connor. He took her hand and then kissed her.

"Do you want chocolate or not?"

"Go. Please go."

"I should probably go, too." Angus took a step

toward the door.

"No, no. You should stay and keep the girls company for a little longer."

"Sit down, Angus." McKayla's voice was firm. "We have to soak up enough Angus time to last us a while."

I could have kissed Connor and McKayla.

Angus sat in the chair Connor had put right beside mine.

"I think he's trying to open his eyes," I said, and instinctively Angus leaned closer to look at him. I could feel the heat of his arm next to mine. I turned the baby a little so Angus could better see his face. "Have you picked a name?"

"We've picked a first name, but we have different ideas about the middle name."

"What are they?"

"His first name is Simon."

"I love it."

"I like Wendell for the middle name."

"Ah, after Grandpa."

"That's the problem. Connor wants to use his grandpa's name. Ellis."

"Simon Wendell Ward. Simon Ellis Ward." Angus tried out both names. "That's tough. They both sound good."

I peeked under the little blue hat at the silky, dark hair. "I guess you need to have another boy."

"Give me a few days to recover, please." For the first time, I noticed a weariness behind McKayla's excitement.

"You look amazing," I said. "I can't believe you had a baby today."

"Thanks."

"Has anyone else been here yet?"

"Dad and Mom were here earlier. Will and Gina are coming later tonight. Connor's mom and dad won't be here 'til tomorrow."

We talked for another half hour before Angus shifted in his seat.

"I should get going. I'm glad I got to meet Simon before I leave."

"Me too," McKayla said. "Thanks for driving over."

Angus leaned over and gave McKayla a hug. She gave me a stern look over his shoulder.

"I know you've got to head back, too, Charlotte, so this is probably a good time for me to try to feed him."

I wasn't eager to hand Simon over, but I understood what McKayla was doing. Angus looked a little trapped, but I didn't care.

"I love him already," I said as I carefully handed him to his mother and then hugged McKayla over the top of him.

"Thanks for coming, you two. Have a safe trip, Angus."

We walked in silence to the elevator. I took a deep breath and let it out slowly. "Only eight days until you leave." I kept my eyes anchored on the changing numbers above the door, pretending I didn't know he was leaving sooner than he'd told me.

"Actually, I'm leaving Monday."

"You are?"

"I had to pay rent for the whole month of August, so I decided I might as well go a little earlier and get settled in before I get so busy."

"Oh. That makes sense."

The elevator doors opened and a man with a bundle of perfectly behaved balloons stepped off.

"You haven't forgotten dinner, I hope." I pushed the button for the lobby.

"Charlotte, I just—"

"No, Angus." I hoped my voice didn't sound as desperate

as I felt. "Please don't say you can't." He didn't say anything. "Please."

Angus sighed and shoved his hands in his pockets. "Tomorrow night?"

My heart broke a little at his response. He didn't sound happy at all. He sounded like someone ready to plow through an unpleasant task to get it over with. My pride wanted to tell him to forget the whole thing, but I didn't. How could I change his mind if I didn't see him?

"Tomorrow's great," I said with enough enthusiasm for both of us.

"Luigi's?"

"No way. Neither of us need therapy." That was a lie. "Let's go somewhere different. Since you're leaving, let me surprise you. It'll be fun."

"I'll drive. I don't feel like contorting myself into your car." Angus smiled. It was so lovely, I felt a clutch in my stomach.

We stepped out into the angled, evening sunshine and hesitated on the sidewalk. "Where's your car?" Angus asked.

"It's over there."

"Do you want me to walk you?"

"That's okay, it's still light." As soon as the words were out of my mouth, I wanted to take them back. I needed to take advantage of every minute I had with him.

"All right. I'll see you tomorrow."

"See you."

Angus didn't move when I started walking away. I crossed the road and found my car in the visitor parking lot. I glanced back to see which way Angus had gone, but he was still standing there watching me. It wasn't until I waved that he turned and walked away.

Chapter 4

Angus

C harles was killing me. Whole hours could pass without her popping into my mind, but sitting beside her in the hospital, little Simon in her arms, had been agony. It wasn't easy to be reminded of what we'd never have. And now she'd roped me into a pointless dinner that I had no idea how to handle. She'd looked so hopeful and eager when she'd suggested we go somewhere new. If we hadn't been friends for so long, I'd have told her no. I'd have said goodbye there on the sidewalk in front of the hospital.

"You ready?" I said into my cell phone. I was parked at the curb in front of her apartment.

"Yes. I'll be right down."

Less than a minute later, there was Charles. She looked amazing. Really gorgeous. I'd never seen the light blue dress she was wearing and I hated that she'd probably gone out and bought it just for tonight. I needed her not to try to impress me. I couldn't allow her to draw me in again.

Six months ago, I'd have been psyched to see her wanting to look good for me. Six months ago I'd been hers for the taking. Now I was leaving for four years, and no matter how obvious it was that she'd be a willing participant in a long-distance relationship, there was no way I was going there. Charles had never demonstrated that she had staying power.

That probably wasn't fair. She'd dated a few punks along the way and I couldn't blame her that they hadn't worked out. But lately I'd started to think maybe she was partly at fault. Kyle would have married her, but she broke it off with him. I didn't know everything that had happened in Scotland, but I was pretty sure Chuck was the reason it hadn't gone anywhere. And then there was me. If she really wanted love and marriage and all the things she claimed she was looking for, I'd been here all along. Sure, she'd had her heart broken several times, but she'd also done her share of damage. Maybe it wasn't always the guys' fault. Maybe Charles had issues I'd overlooked because I was in love with her. I certainly had no evidence that she could make a four-year, long-distance relationship work, and I had too much to worry about to set myself up for a bigger disappointment down the road. This guy was moving on. This next four years was about getting over Charles so I could create a life with someone who wouldn't rip my heart into chunks the way she had.

She smiled and turned to lock her front door.

I looked away. No way was she going to do it to me again, no matter how great she looked, no matter how pretty her eyes were. I just had to get through the evening and then I'd be on my way. I couldn't let her overtake my life and my thoughts again.

"Hey," I said after I leaned across the car and opened the door for her.

Charles smiled. "I hope you're hungry."

"I am. Where are we going, boss?"

She looked proud of herself. "I got reservations at Cashmere."

"Charles, no." Cashmere was way too expensive. I didn't want her to spend so much on a futile evening.

"What? You're going far away for a long time. This is your going away dinner. I want it to be nice."

"We'll go Dutch," I said, even though I knew I couldn't afford it.

"No we won't. I invited you, and this is my treat." She was blushing a little.

Part of me wanted to reassure her, to tell her I'd feel more comfortable at Luigi's or even McDonalds, but I didn't want to argue with her. And I recognized the stubborn look on her face. It was the same look she'd had when Will and I had told her she couldn't play football with us in junior high. She'd insisted she could and had tackled Will so hard she'd knocked the wind out of him.

"If you're sure."

"I am."

I'd never been to Cashmere before, had never even entertained the thought of eating there. It was the kind of place the wealthy went to be seen and people like us went to propose or to celebrate a huge promotion. The place was wasted on an evening like ours, and it became even clearer what Charlotte was trying to accomplish tonight. I should have found an excuse to cancel. This wasn't fair to her.

I thought I might be underdressed, but when we arrived, I saw a few others in khakis and button-down shirts so I wasn't out of place. And Charles fit in just fine. She may not have looked quite as made up as some of the other women in the restaurant, but she was definitely the prettiest.

Charlotte's eyes grew large when she opened the menu, but she recovered quickly. "Get whatever you want."

I ordered a chicken salad. There was one other meal that cost less, but I didn't want to make it obvious that I was trying to go cheap. A waiter delivered a steak to the next table that made my mouth water, but no way was I going to let Chuck spend as much on dinner as I'd spend on gas all the way to Missouri.

Chuck ordered an appetizer because "she wasn't all that hungry and wanted to save room for dessert."

I had to admit my chicken salad was good. There was some kind of spice on the meat that I didn't recognize, but I wished I could have seconds.

I interrupted when the waiter asked if we wanted dessert. I know Charles. She likes dessert, but I didn't want her to blow her next week's food budget on a credit card-sized piece of cheesecake. "Hey, you treated me to dinner. Let's go to Marigold's. I'll treat you to the chocolate chip cookie pie."

One word about that pie and Charlotte's stubborn streak was tamed. "Mmm, that does sound good." She turned to the waiter. "I think we're finished. Thank you."

He bowed as he stepped away from the table, and Charlotte smiled at me. Why did she have to be so cute?

Marigold's was much more comfortable, and Chuck was in a good mood. It probably had something to do with the pie. Up until now we'd been actively avoiding the reason for our dinner, but now Charles wanted to know everything.

"What's a hip fellowship, anyway?"

"It means I'll be getting some focused experience working with hips. By the time I'm finished, I'll be a specialist, so other orthopedists will consult with me when they have a patient having problems with their hips."

We took a few bites of dessert. "Are you nervous?" she asked.

I shrugged. "I guess a little. But mostly I'm excited. There's finally an end in sight."

"Four years sounds like a lot to me. Sorry, that wasn't a very encouraging thing to say."

"I get it. But after nine years, four doesn't sound so bad."

"I guess it's all about perspective."

A toddler in the booth behind Charlotte was throwing a temper tantrum. He cried and kicked the back of Charlotte's seat. He got more and more upset until finally, the father put him over his shoulder and carried him outside. The mom put a few bills on the table and followed him, stopping at our table.

"I'm so sorry about that."

Charles waved her off. "Don't worry about it. Even throwing a fit, he's adorable." She had always been good at making people feel more comfortable.

A few years ago, I had a professor whose wife had multiple sclerosis and he'd offered extra credit to any student who ran an MS 5K. Never being one to let an extra credit opportunity pass me by, of course I entered the race. Chuck had offered to run it with me to keep me company. Right after we crossed the finish line, when she was hot and winded and bent over, propping herself up on her knees, some guy had come up to her.

"Hi, Charlotte."

She'd looked up at him, sideways. "Pete. How's it going?"

"Good." He'd shuffled his feet and barely lifted his eyes from the ground. "Listen, sorry I was such a jerk. I should have called you to let you know where things stood."

"Don't worry about it."

"It was a lousy thing to do. Liz said she wanted to give us

another chance, and I just . . . I don't know. I should have told you."

"Pete. Really, it's not a big deal. We weren't going to happen anyway, so you probably did us both a favor. No hard feelings."

Pete looked like he'd been cured of a terminal illness. He finally lifted his eyes to look at Chuck. "Well, it's good to see you."

"You, too."

"I'm glad I saw you today. I've wanted to talk to you for a long time."

"Well now you have, so go be happy and don't worry about me."

"Thanks, Charlotte. Take care."

"Bye, Pete."

"I thought you liked him," I said when he was gone.

"I did."

"So what was that?"

"It's over. There's no need for him to beat himself up over it for the next ten years."

I felt a little twinge of guilt that I'd been so hard on Charles the last few months. She may have let me down, but she was a great person. I'd seen her kindness many times over the years.

Our dessert was gone but we didn't immediately get up to leave. Charles slid her plate to the end of the table, clasped her hands, and leaned forward. "Angus, I want you to know I'm sorry."

I turned my fork over and over on the table, trying not to make eye contact. "For what?"

"For a lot of things. I'm sorry I set you up with Aleena. I thought I was doing a good thing, but I wasn't. I didn't mean for it to be hard for either of you."

I nodded, and she continued. "I'm sorry about the way I handled everything after my birthday. I wish I could go back and do things differently, but I can't."

"Don't feel bad. Things happen for a reason." She sighed and leaned back against the booth. It was hard for me not to think about all the times we'd sat in a similar booth at Luigi's, helping each other through the ups and downs of dating. "You'll be okay, Chuck."

She bit the side of her mouth. "You think?"

"Don't feel bad that I'm leaving. This is a good thing."

"Maybe for you."

"For both of us. It will make it easier for us to move on and find the right thing." I ignored the frustrated look that passed over Charlotte's face. "You were a good friend, Chuck."

Charlotte's shoulders stiffened. "Why are you saying that in past tense? It's like one of us is dying or something."

I smiled but she didn't smile back. "Not dying. Just leaving."

"I don't want you to talk in past tense." She looked like she might start crying and I knew that would be a disaster. I always get protective when Chuck cries, and how could I protect her from me?

"Okay." I wouldn't upset her, even though tonight would soon be over and everything about *us* would become past tense.

"Let's go," she said. I could tell she was flustered.

We walked around the corner to my car. Chuck's arms were folded tightly, like she was trying to ward off a chill even though it wasn't cold.

I couldn't find a parking place on Charlotte's street and I wasn't about to drop her off and wave goodbye when this was it. The end. Sure, we'd see each other again, but I knew our circumstances would probably be much different then. Chuck would probably be married by the time I moved back. If I moved back. Maybe I would be, too. I parked the car and we walked slowly back to her door.

"Thanks for dinner, Chuck. I thought I'd die before I ever ate at Cashmere."

"Sure."

Charles looked nervous. I wasn't sure what else to say, so I lifted my hand to wave goodbye. The next thing I knew, Charlotte's arms were around me. I loosely hugged her back. "Be safe," she said into my shoulder.

"I will." Her hair smelled good and I took a deep breath.

Charlotte was the first to pull back, and I felt a moment of relief. And then her hands were on my jaws and her lips were pressed against mine. I stiffened. I don't know why I hadn't seen this coming. She kissed me twice and then a third time, soft gentle kisses that ate away at my resolve.

"Don't, Chuck." I took a small step back, but she didn't let go. She held me there with her hands, shaking her head, which only made it so her lips brushed over mine several times, softly at first and then a little more insistent.

If she was trying to wear me down, it was working. Boy was it working.

I wrapped one arm around her waist and buried the other hand under her hair at her neck and kissed her back, hungry for everything I'd wanted with her. Rational thoughts tried to get through to my brain. "This is a mistake." "What are you doing?" "This won't help you get her out of your system." "She's going to level you again." I shoved them aside and allowed myself to be lost in Charlotte. Lost in her kiss, the way her hair felt on the back of my hand, the feel of her hands on my face and her body in my arms. For a few minutes, I forgot about all the times she'd cut me off at the knees. I forgot about the ache I had felt every time she started dating someone new instead of me. I ignored the memory of her turning her back on me and fleeing to Scotland.

But no matter how much I wanted to stay lost in the moment, I couldn't ignore the warning voices that were clamoring in my head, refusing to be silenced. I took a slow step back. Charlotte was a fire too dangerous to play with. Whether she'd meant to or not, she'd burned me too many times. I'd barely started to put myself back together. I couldn't let it happen again. What if I let her in and she left me the way she'd left Kyle and Braveheart?

"I've got to go."

Charlotte nodded.

"I hope someday you find someone who's perfect for you, Chuck."

She looked like I'd slapped her, and I felt horrible. I couldn't stand the look of disappointment in her eyes, so I turned and walked away.

"I already have," she whispered.

I groaned as I walked to my car. With each step I picked up a piece of the wall I'd just allowed Charlotte to demolish, and carefully began rebuilding it. It didn't matter how much I loved her. It didn't matter how many times she said she was sorry.

Monday couldn't come fast enough. I needed to be on the interstate heading east, driving toward safety, going somewhere far away, where my heart could heal and where Charlotte didn't have the power to destroy me.

Chapter 5

Charlotte

*A*ngus was gone and even though I had only seen him a few times since my return from Scotland, I still felt the loss. It was like the argon had been removed from the atmosphere. Nothing looked different, but everything felt different.

I knew Angus's apartment in Kansas City was small but nicer than he'd expected and that it had a swimming pool he probably wouldn't have time to use. I knew he'd met some of the people he'd be working with and that he didn't know if he could get used to the heat and humidity.

I wished I knew these things because he'd told me, but all my information had come from Will, who told the family at a Labor Day barbecue.

"Does he sound happy?" I asked Will as I dished up potato salad.

"Yeah. He's busy but he sounds good." Will jostled me with his elbow. "Call him, Charles. Or send him an email."

I shrugged. "I don't think he wants to hear from me."

"Of course he wants to hear from you. Stop being dramatic and get in touch with him."

It was easy for Will to say that Angus would want to hear from me. He didn't know about the monumental brushoff Angus had given me. Every time I thought about that night, I wanted a do-over. Things had been good. We'd finally put the awkwardness behind us and Angus had talked to me like we were friends again. And then I'd ruined it. It didn't matter that he'd kissed me back. What mattered was that he'd never felt further from me when he left. I wanted to go back and hug Angus goodbye and then walk into my apartment with my head held high. If I'd done that, I wouldn't have to cringe at the memory. I wouldn't feel so awkward about making a "friendly" phone call or sending a "friendly" text. It felt like that kiss had lit the "friend" ship on fire and shoved it out to burn at sea.

I needed someone to talk to, someone who would let me talk and vent and figure things out. It needed to be someone who wouldn't feel guilty about my situation (Jayne), someone who wasn't best friends with Angus (Will and probably the rest of my family), and someone I hadn't hurt (Aleena and Angus and probably Flynn). I was with my family, people who cared about me and loved me, but I'd never felt so isolated. I could talk to Mia, but I refused to rain on her long-awaited parade.

I smiled and joined in the conversation, but the only time I forgot about my loneliness was when I played with Emily and held Simon while he slept.

Mom hugged me tightly when I left, and I knew she could tell I wasn't okay, but didn't know how to help me. That made it worse. When you think your mother finds your situation hopeless, what have you got left?

Tears flowed as I pulled onto the freeway. I cried all the way home and was glad Mia wasn't there when I arrived. I brushed my teeth and went to bed so I wouldn't risk having to talk to her or Graham. As I lay in bed, I pictured Scarlett O'Hara sitting on the steps, tears in her eyes. I fell asleep to the words, "After all, tomorrow is another day." I wasn't sure if that was good or bad.

It had been nearly three months since I'd talked to Aleena. I was starting to think the damage I'd done to our friendship was irreparable, but I was determined to try one more time before I gave up. Somehow I needed to see her face to face.

I felt like Veronica Mars as I watched the door to Aleena's building. I'd been there more than twenty minutes when a man walked out with a twitchy Chihuahua and headed north. I hurried to the door and caught it before it closed, narrowly escaping a couple of smashed fingers. Once inside the building, I rode the elevator up to the third floor and sat cross-legged against the wall outside her door and waited.

I sat there nearly an hour before the doors to the elevator at the end of the hall opened and Aleena stepped off. When she saw me, she took a step backward and put her hand up to keep the door from closing. I was afraid she might get back on and leave.

I scrambled to my feet and looked at her, my eyes pleading her to stay and talk to me. She held the door until it started beeping and she had to make a choice. Finally, a look of resignation crossed her face and she walked toward me.

I spoke first. "Hi."

"Hi." She brushed past me and unlocked her door. I wasn't sure what to do. I didn't want to follow her, uninvited, into her apartment, but I didn't want her to go in and leave me out in the hall either.

She walked inside and I stood there while the door swung closed in front of me. It clicked shut and I waited, wondering if this meant she wanted me to leave. I was about to knock when the door opened wide. "Well, get in here if you're coming."

I quickly stepped inside.

"Hi." It was difficult to keep my voice from quivering.

"Yeah. You said that."

"Aleena, can we please talk?"

She sighed and her voice changed from cross to sad. "I let you in, didn't I? Come in and sit down."

I sat on her purple, crushed velvet couch. Aleena sat in the farthest chair. I didn't know if that was intentional or not, but it made me even more nervous. When it became clear that she wasn't going to start the conversation, I finally spoke.

"I'm so sorry. I don't know what else to say."

Aleena sat with perfect posture, her hands in her lap, her face unreadable. "You really didn't know he was in love with you?"

"I had no idea."

"Do you love him?"

I nodded.

Aleena sighed. "I don't mean like a friend. I mean are you in love with him?"

"I am. But I didn't know that either."

Aleena smiled a sad smile, and her shoulders relaxed a

little. "For a girl who's dated as much as you have, you're not very perceptive."

I was so relieved to see her smile, even if it didn't look happy. "What do you mean?"

"Oh, Charlotte. You were right. He's amazing. He's such a good guy that I fell for him in spite of everything."

I was confused. "In spite of what?"

"I could tell you two had a thing. I wasn't sure what was going on, but . . . I don't know." I wanted to ask her what she meant, but I didn't want to upset her, so I stayed quiet. Then she continued. "He was always talking about you."

"He was?"

Aleena rolled her eyes. "I mean, I get it. You're good friends, but enough about Chuck already."

I felt a little thrill at the thought of Angus talking about me, but then I remembered things had changed, and right now it didn't matter how much he'd said about me then.

"And then there was that time when we were at your brother's and you were watching Emily and you got all weird when I kissed him, and even though he'd been fine kissing me other times, he seemed embarrassed that you'd seen it." She sighed. "And there were other things, too, but I tried to ignore them."

"I was so clueless. I knew things were awkward sometimes, but I didn't understand why."

Aleena laughed a little. "You really are ridiculous. I've always had to point out the obvious to you."

"Yeah. I guess I am."

"You know what they say. 'It's a foolish, foolish girl who refuses to see what's right in front of her.'"

"Who says that?"

Aleena shrugged. "I don't know. I'm sure someone has said it. Maybe it was Confucius."

I shook my head. "Aleena, please forgive me. I don't know how I can survive without your made up proverbs and fortunes."

Aleena smiled. "I forgive you. I was just so disappointed. But I guess I should be glad at least one of us can have him."

I picked at a thread on my jeans. "I don't have him."

Aleena looked surprised. "What are you talking about? He told me he was in love with you."

"He did?"

"Well, he said he was in love with someone else. I'd have to be an idiot not to know who he was talking about."

"He told me it's too late. He's gone. He moved to Kansas City."

Aleena looked stunned. "Why would he give up someone like me if he wasn't ready to sweep you off your feet?" She smiled and moved to the couch. I almost sobbed. We were going to be okay.

"Aleena, I'm not sure why anyone would give you up for anything."

Aleena pulled her legs up under her and leaned toward me. "So what now?"

"I have no idea. Let me know if you come up with any brilliant ideas."

"I'll give it some thought. And Charlotte?"

"Yes?"

"I love you, but please don't ever set me up again."

I put up my hands in surrender. "Never again. I promise."

Chapter 6

Charlotte

*I*t's hard to explain the relief I felt at having finally cleared the air with Aleena. I still didn't have the friend I'd had before. Maybe someday I'd be able to ask Aleena's opinion on what I should do to solve the Angus problem, but right now our truce was too fresh, too fragile. Maybe we'd never get to a place where we'd be able to speak freely about dating in general and Angus in particular.

I turned on my computer when I arrived at the office one morning to find an email from Flynn mixed in with all the work emails.

To: ce@jaynefife.com

From: flynnmac@scotnet.co.uk

Time: 12:13 p.m.

Re: Greetings!

I'll be mighty disappointed if I don't get an invite to your wedding. Hope you're well. Perhaps Skype would be in order? Tomorrow morning? (unless you're tasting wedding cakes or picking out flowers, of course) –Flynn

I smiled. Even though it meant having to confess the uncertainty of my future, I was excited to talk to Flynn. I was suddenly eager to hear his perspective.

To: flynnmac@scotnet.co.uk

From: ce@jaynefife.com

Time: 1:39 p.m.

Re: Greetings!

If I ever marry, you'll definitely be invited. Things didn't go according to plan, but I'm adapting. Sort of. Skype is definitely in order. Can't wait.

Charlotte

The computer signaled a call and I hurried into the living room. I settled into the corner of the couch as the call connected.

"Charlotte, how are ya?"

41

"Look at your face." The stubble I was used to had turned into a full beard.

"Gettin' ready for the winter." Flynn ran his hand over his beard.

"You grow it out every year?"

"Got to keep those vicious north winds out."

Flynn smiled and I melted. I had needed someone to talk to for so long. Why had I thought I couldn't talk to Flynn? One minute in and I already knew he was exactly what I needed to help me figure out my life.

"It definitely looks warm. Is it already cold there?"

"Naw, but it's right around the corner. Let's not talk about the weather. Tell me what happened with you. Why are you having to adapt?"

I sighed. "Oh, Flynn. Nothing went the way it was supposed to. I had such a good plan, but it didn't work." I told him everything that had transpired with Angus when I returned home. It was embarrassing, but I even included the kiss goodbye. He asked a few questions, but mostly he listened and his eyes were kind and thoughtful. "And now he's gone. He lives half a continent away and there's nothing I can do to fix things."

"Ah, Charlotte, I'm sorry. I thought you'd be gettin' married about now."

I laughed. "That would have been fast. But I certainly didn't picture this mess when I came home."

"What're ya plannin' to do?"

"I'll wait. I love him."

"Four years is a long time."

"So long."

"Sad Charlotte. Maybe you should come back to Stornoway while ya wait."

"Don't tempt me. That place is heaven. I was so sure of

42

everything while I was there."

"Ya weren't sure of everything. You were just sure of yourself."

I nodded. "I miss that. Right now I don't have any idea what I'm doing." Flynn ran his hand through his hair. "You wouldn't want to give up your house again anyway."

"Aye, but I would if ya came. Or ya could stay with mum. But your problems won't be solved here."

I groaned. "Enough about me. How are you? How is your mum?"

"Mum's good. She keeps askin' after ya."

"Tell her I'm fine."

"I will."

"I really am fine. Did you finish the Crawford's house?"

"Aye, it's a pretty one. I told him if he ever decides to sell, I want first shot at it."

"Did you take pictures?"

"I did."

"You should send them to me."

"I shoulda thought of that. Ya built the chimney, after all."

"Not really. But I'd love to see it."

We talked a little longer, but it was late there and I could tell Flynn was tired.

"You're a brave lass, Charlotte. You'll figure out what to do."

"I hope so." I paused. "Thank you for calling me, Flynn. You have no idea how much I needed this."

"We've missed ya here."

I swallowed. "I miss all of you, too. Please say hello to your mum and Jessie. Good night, Flynn."

"Good morning, Charlotte."

We were both smiling when we disconnected the call.

My phone rang before six the next morning. Who would call that early on a Sunday? I rubbed my bleary eyes and looked at the screen. The number was unfamiliar and a strange configuration. I almost shut it off, but on a hunch, I answered the call.

"Charlotte, it's Flynn."

"Flynn? Is everything okay?"

"Aye. I think we should talk. Turn on your computer and call me."

Ten minutes later, Flynn appeared on the screen of my laptop.

"What's going on?"

"I think you should move to Kansas City."

I laughed. "What are you talking about?"

"Don't laugh. I'm not jokin'."

"I can't move to Kansas City. My job's here. My family's here. And I don't think Angus would even want me to."

"Ah, he'd say he doesn't want ya to, but I'd wager that what he wants and what he says he wants are two different things."

I shook my head. "You're crazy. This is what you wanted me to call you for at this hour of the morning?"

"Aye. And hear me out. I've been chewin' on this all day."

I was touched that he'd been trying to figure out a way to help me, but this idea was insane. "I'm listening."

"You say you'll wait for him to come back." I nodded. "What about him? You might be willing to wait for ten years, but what about Angus? He'll be meeting new people. He won't be waiting around. If ya want to cook a chicken, ya have to put him in while the water's boilin'."

I snickered. "I don't even know what that means, Flynn."

"Sure ya do. If ya wait 'til the water's all cooled down, good luck cooking the bird. Right now the water's boilin'."

"No it's not. He doesn't want anything to do with me."

"That's 'cause the water's boilin'. If it weren't, he'd talk to ya all day long. He's just tryin' not to get burned."

There was an absurd and comforting logic to what he was saying. "Keep going."

"There's not much more to say. Move to Kansas City."

"That's easier said than done, Flynn."

"Tell me this. What needs more attention? The things in San Francisco? Or the thing in Kansas City?"

I didn't answer him. I didn't know what to say.

"Charlotte, give him a grand gesture. Show 'im he's more important than the things you've left behind."

"Wow. I should never have answered the phone this morning."

We laughed. "Think about it. It might work."

"It might not. And then I'll be two thousand miles away from my family and I'll have given up the best job in the world and . . . It's all so scary."

"But you're brave. And if it doesn't work out, you can go back."

"I thought you were my friend."

Flynn didn't say anything right away. He just smiled. When he finally spoke, his voice was soft. "I am."

Chapter 7

Charlotte

Flynn had stewed on my problem for a day. I stewed on it for a week, and the longer I did, the more convinced I became that Flynn was right. Everything he'd said rang true.

The problem was me. I was terrified.

To go to Kansas City, I'd have to give up my apartment and my job. I'd have to face family and friends who would surely think I'd lost my mind. Would my car even make it that far?

And what about Angus? He'd made it clear he was through with me. What would he do if he found out I was following him halfway across the country? I couldn't imagine him being happy about it. Wasn't this what you'd call putting all your eggs in one basket?

If I did this crazy thing, I'd be putting every one of my eggs in the Angus basket. Of course I was scared. Angus had already tossed that basket in the trash.

I wasn't sure where to start. Should I tell my parents first? I pictured making the rounds, first to Dad and Mom's, then Will and Gina's and McKayla and Connor's. The conversations I imagined taking place during those visits were enough to add an extra two or three days to my consideration.

I'd been working at my desk most of the morning when I realized I had no idea what I'd been sketching. My subconscious obviously knew I was supposed to be painting a giraffe for a mug, because it looked pretty good, but I couldn't remember a single brush stroke. My mind scampered all over the place—to my conversation with Flynn, to my parents, to cute little Emily and sweet Simon who would hardly know me if I left.

But mostly my mind traveled to Kansas City, a place I'd never been. My best friend was there. The man I loved. I missed him. I missed the easiness of our conversations and the way we could count on each other. I missed his smile and his teasing. I even missed the awful nicknames. My birthday had given me something else to miss. I missed Angus's kiss. I missed his strong arms.

The thought that I might have lost everything about Angus fired me up and I made my decision.

Suddenly my chair was a black, Angus-less hole and I bolted up with such fervor to escape it, I nearly knocked it over behind me. I took a deep breath and walked with determination to Jayne's office.

"Hi, Charlotte."

I stepped inside, closed the door and sat in the chair opposite her. She looked concerned and I glanced around the room to avoid eye contact. "I've never told you how much I like your office." I ran my hand over the chrome arm of the chair. "It just looks like it belongs to someone artistic, you know? I mean, who but an artist would have chartreuse chairs? Who but an artist would even know what chartreuse is?"

"Thanks?" She said the word slowly. "Did you close the door so we could speak freely about my color choices?"

I laughed, and Jayne smiled, though she still looked worried.

"No. I just thought I should mention it before I leave."

Jayne's face morphed from confusion to panic. "Leave?"

"Jayne, I have to move. To Kansas City."

"What are you talking about? What's in Kansas City?"

I took a deep breath and let it out slowly. A reassuring calm settled over me. I knew that would probably pass and I'd be faced with my own sense of panic, but I would use the peace I felt at the moment to get as much done as I could.

"Angus is there. He's finishing his residency in Kansas City, and . . . well, I want to be where he is."

"The Angus that's like your brother? The one you eat out with after you break up? Kyle's fiancé's ex? Him?"

I nodded. "Him."

I spent the next several minutes bringing Jayne up to speed.

"I was right then. Something has been bothering you."

"Yes. But I wasn't ready to say anything. I didn't think I could do anything about it, so why moan? But now I know I can. And I am."

"What about work? What will you do there?"

"I hope I can find something. I've got a little money saved. I don't really know what I'll do, but it doesn't matter. I'll wait tables if I have to or clean hotel rooms. I just know I need to go." Now that I'd made this decision, I was even more grateful that Flynn had insisted I stay at his house and save the money I would have spent on a hotel when I traveled to Scotland.

Jayne collapsed back in her chair. I gave her some time for it to sink in.

"I hate for you to go, but I guess I understand." She was quiet again. "Let's talk in the morning. Maybe you'll have changed your mind."

I shook my head. "I won't have. I'm sorry . . ."

Jayne put up her hand to stop me. "I can't think about this right now. Let's talk in the morning."

I wanted to say more, but the look on Jayne's face stopped me.

When I got back to my office, I sent a group text to my family.

Me: When's the soonest everyone can meet at Dad and Mom's?

McKayla: Why?

Gina: Is everything okay?

My phone rang at the same time that a text from Will flashed on the screen. I glanced at it before I answered the phone.

Will: I get off at 5:30 every night. Do we have anything this week, Gina?

I answered the phone.

"Charlotte?" It was Mom.

"Hi, Mom."

"Are you okay?"

"I'm fine. I just need to tell the family something and I wanted to do it all at the same time. And not over the phone."

"What is it?" Mom sounded equal parts concerned and curious.

I smiled. "It's okay, Mom. You don't need to worry."

I knew that wasn't entirely true.

"You're not going to tell me, are you?"

"Of course I am. When the family is together."

"Oh, all right. I hope everyone can come tonight. I'd better go so I can encourage everyone."

"Love you, Mom."

"I love you too, honey."

Two texts were waiting when I hung up.

Gina: We were going to my sister's for dinner on Friday, but other than that we don't have anything. Charlotte, are you coming alone? wink wink

McKayla: Connor? Any conflicts?

Mom wasted no time sending a text to the group.

Mom: If you can all come tonight, Dad and I will order pizza.

Me: I'll be alone.

Will: We can come tonight.

McKayla: I called Connor and we can come tonight.

Mom: Great! We'll order pizza about 7. Does that work for everyone? Charlotte? Can you make it tonight?

Me: haha. Yes, I can. Seven is good.

McKayla: This better be good or we're all going to be disappointed.

Will: Sorry we're such a slacker family and you're having to stage your own intervention, Chuck.

Me: Yeah, thanks a lot guys.

Will: For the record, I've been meaning to talk to you about your Housewives of Escondido addiction.

Me: Ew.

McKayla: How do you know this isn't an intervention for you, Will?

Gina: Shhh. You weren't supposed to tell him.

Will: On second thought, I'm not sure we can make it. Remember that thing we have tonight, Gina?

Gina: Nice try, Will. See you all tonight.

McKayla: I've been craving some chocolate chip cookies, so I'll make some this afternoon.

Connor: Save me some dough.

McKayla: So now you join the conversation. I guess I should have mentioned cookie dough a long time ago.

Connor: Sorry. I was working. But I'm excited for an intervention.

Me: Thanks everyone. See you all tonight.

I spent my lunch hour at my computer, taking a crash course on Kansas City. According to the chamber of commerce, it was a vibrant city with flourishing suburban communities and lovely tree-lined streets. A downtown plaza boasted the highest-rated Christmas light display in the country and the cost of living was significantly less than the Bay area. That was good news.

The few minutes I spent looking at rental properties showed plenty of options, ranging from large and jam-packed with amenities to basic and pretty affordable. Without a waiting job, the less expensive options were definitely at the top of my list. I saved a couple of the more affordable ones to my favorites so I could make some phone calls in the next few days.

The last few minutes of my lunch were spent looking for

graphic design jobs. I was glad I needed to get back to work. The thought of leaving my dream job and starting somewhere new made my heart hurt and I didn't want to disintegrate into a pile of sadness and tears. Today, when I was about to face my entire family, I had to be focused and determined. There was no place for indecision and weakness.

The afternoon flew by. I couldn't leave the Sunset Safari Wild Animal Park mid-project. The couple of other campaigns I had coming up weren't started yet and could easily be taken on by someone else, but I was about half finished with Sunset Safari, and now that I had made my decision, I wanted to make the move as soon as possible, before my courage faltered.

My Volkswagen Bug hummed and rattled as I took the onramp to I-80 toward Fairfield, and it occurred to me that my cute, little car was a concern. Didn't Kansas City get a lot of snow? Oh man. I was headed to a cold climate right before winter and I had never been a fan of freezing temperatures. I've only driven in the snow twice in my life and one of those times I'd lost control and slid hard into a curb.

"I wish you were a four-wheel drive," I said to my car and patted the dashboard.

It was a wimpy thing to do, but when I pulled up to the house and saw that only Will and Gina's car was there, I drove on. I didn't want to be pelted with questions before everyone had arrived. I drove slowly, looking at the familiar neighborhood. I stopped across the street from the house where Angus had grown up. So many memories lived there. Janice and Dave Barclay had been like second parents to Will and me. When I got tired of playing NBA video games with Will and Angus, I'd kept Janice company. Dave had teased me about being one of the guys, but if they ever started to roughhouse with me, he'd remind them I was a lady.

The basketball hoop above the garage was gone, which made me a little sad. I rarely played with them, but I'd sit on the grass, my back against the walnut tree in their front yard, and sketch pictures while they played. Suddenly, my eyes burned and nostalgia squeezed my throat and chest. I wanted to go back to the time we were best friends and almost every day was spent together. I didn't just miss Angus. I missed all of us, the kids that could fight and forgive in minutes, the trio who always had each other's backs. If I could go back, I'd watch for the clues that things were different. I'd be ready when our feelings started to change, and I'd never, never, never be the one who caused Angus pain.

I had to have Angus back in my life. I had to make things right no matter what it took.

Chapter 8

Charlotte

"Better hurry before they eat it all." The young deliveryman was getting in his car as I arrived.

"That would serve me right for being the last to arrive."

He smiled and waved as he drove off. I took a deep breath and blew it out slowly, steeling myself for whatever opposition I might face about this rash and possibly irresponsible plan I was presenting.

"She's here," Will said when I stepped into the kitchen.

"Thanks for waiting for me," I joked, watching my family loading up slices of pizza and breadsticks.

"It just got here," Mom assured me.

"I know. I passed him in the driveway."

"Everyone get your food and let's go sit down so Charlotte can share her news," Mom said.

"She might want to eat first." Dad winked at me.

"You eat while I talk." I'd have trouble choking down my

food until I got this off my chest. "Then I'll eat while you tell me how crazy I am."

The room fell silent and everyone turned to look at me. I tried to laugh but it came off more like a goat yodeling. "It was a joke." I turned and headed for the living room. "Sort of."

I don't think my family has ever assembled and quieted themselves so quickly. Within three minutes, all eyes were expectantly on me.

"Whew. This is hard." I sat in a swivel chair close to the fireplace. I pivoted the chair back and forth, my nerves making it difficult to sit still. Just a few feet away was the place Angus had pulled me into his arms and told me how he felt.

I planted my feet firmly on the floor to stop my momentum and sat up straight.

"I have a few things to tell you and it isn't going to be easy. Please let me get it all out before you jump on me and try to talk me out of it, okay?" When no one spoke, I swallowed hard and continued. "I'm in love with Angus."

"No kidding," McKayla said softly, and Connor shushed her. It seemed everyone was trying to suppress little smiles. Except Mom. There was no attempt to hide her delight. She was quietly patting Dad's leg over and over until he took her hand and held it still in his own.

I grinned. "Wow. So I guess this came as a bigger shock to me than it did to all of you."

"We're not as blind as you are," Will said.

"Be quiet," Gina whispered.

"Then you probably won't be too surprised when I tell you I'm moving to Kansas City."

You'd have thought I'd dropped a shock bomb on the room, and only Will was immune to its mood-altering effects. His smile was like a gift. My eyes met his and he gave me a little nod that filled me with courage.

"You think this is a good idea?" I'm sure Mom didn't mean for her voice to sound so accusing when she turned on Will.

Will's smile didn't falter. "Absolutely. They love each other. She should be where he is."

"I didn't even know you two had started dating," Dad said.

"We haven't." All eyes were back on me. "I mean . . . we're not exactly dating."

"What does 'not exactly dating' mean?" Mom looked confused.

"It means we haven't been dating. But I know he loves me, or he did a few months ago. And I know I love him, and if I don't go, who knows what will happen. He's going to be gone a long time and . . . I don't want him to forget me."

"If it's right, he won't forget you," Mom said, panic rising in her voice.

"Come on, Mom." Will's voice was gentle. "That kind of thinking might have been reasonable when Chuck was eighteen or something. But we're twenty-seven years old now. If she loves him, she'd be nuts to wait around hoping it's right for four years."

I loved that Will had said "we're twenty-seven." It had never been "I" with us. We had always been a team, and that solidarity bolstered my confidence.

"If you two wanted to test the waters, why did he leave?" Dad asked. "Why didn't he finish his residency here?"

It was a reasonable question, but there was so much history I didn't plan to share. They didn't need to know he'd taken the Kansas City fellowship and residency to get away from me. They didn't need to know that he'd rejected me. Twice. Those things would only make them think I was crazy

56

to follow him, and I needed their support. Or if not their support, at least their quiet resignation to my plan.

"This was a good opportunity for him. He had to take it," Will said, and I wondered how much he knew of our situation.

"You can understand why we hate the idea of you moving so far away," Dad said. "But I'm sure Angus will help you get settled in and make sure you're okay."

I glanced at Will. Part of me wanted to leave it there and have my family think Angus was on board with my move and would look after me when I arrived. But that wouldn't have been honest, and I couldn't stand the idea of leaving my family without telling them the truth.

"Angus doesn't know I'm coming." I looked at Will for support as gasps and horror filled the room.

"I think surprising him is a great idea," he said.

"Maybe you should be thinking more of your sister and less of your best friend," Mom said. Mom didn't usually lash out like this, and I felt bad, but grateful, that Will had put himself in front of the speeding train that was Mom's concern.

"You know better than that, Mom." Will's voice was firm. "I would never, ever choose Angus over Charlotte. It's because I love Charlotte that I want her to be happy, and there isn't a person in this room that doesn't know those two belong together. And let's be honest—sorry Chuck," he said to me. "Charlotte has yanked Angus around for years. It's about time she came around. And it's going to take a big move to show him she's serious. I think she's on the right track."

The room was quiet. I was glad Will was on my side, and even though his words were true, they were a knife jabbing at my heart.

"I'm going." My voice was quiet. "I hope I go with everyone's support and prayers, but even if you disapprove, I'm going."

"Can you at least let him know you're coming?" Dad asked. "So he can help you get situated and moved in."

I shook my head. "He'll tell me not to come."

McKayla handed baby Simon to Connor and crossed the room to hug me. "I hate that you're moving, but I totally get it. I love you both, and you should be together."

"Thank you," I whispered in her ear.

McKayla wiped a tear from her cheek as she sat back down by Connor and pulled the baby back onto her lap.

"Mom." Will was doing his best to help Mom accept what I was doing. "Angus has been waiting on Charles for years. He'll take good care of her."

"He doesn't even know she's coming." Mom's voice broke on the words.

"He'll know soon enough," Dad said and put his arm around her.

"How soon are you going?" Connor asked.

"As soon as I can get everything arranged."

"You're not going to Kansas City in the Bug," Dad said.

"I was wondering about that on the way here."

For more than an hour, we talked about plans and logistics. Everyone joined in the conversation except Mom, who listened and picked at the fringe on a gray throw until I thought it might fall apart in her hands.

McKayla and Connor left first. McKayla hugged me and held both my hands. "He'll be so glad you've come."

"I want to believe that, but what if he doesn't want me there?" I spoke quietly so Mom and Dad wouldn't hear me.

"Then you'll have to change his mind."

Will and Gina left next. "You're so brave," Gina said as she hugged me.

"Not really. I'm scared to death," I whispered. "But don't

tell Mom. That's the last thing she needs to know."

Gina squeezed my hand. "She's scared, too. She's worried about you."

"I know."

"Good girl, Chuck." Will hugged me.

"You should have told me how he felt a long time ago."

"Sometimes I wondered. But it wasn't my secret to share. Let me know if you need anything."

I took the empty pizza boxes to the trash can outside. When I came back in, Dad was patting Mom's back and she quickly wiped her cheeks.

"I'm sorry, Mom. I hate to worry you like this."

Mom mustered a small smile and shook her head. "You know, I hardly had to worry about you at all when most parents were worrying about their kids. But you've more than made up for it the last year or so." She laughed. "Scotland. Kansas City. Running off by yourself all the time."

I hardly thought two times counted as all the time, but I'd allow Mom some worried mother exaggerations.

"I'm sorry." I crossed the kitchen and we hugged each other. "I have to go."

Mom nodded against my shoulder.

Dad was leaning against the counter, his arms folded. "Let's meet tomorrow after work. Your mom and I will go with you to trade in your car for something safer, and we'll get some dinner."

"Sounds good." Suddenly I knew if I didn't leave, I'd cry in front of my parents. That would only compound their concern. "I've got a big day ahead of me tomorrow."

I had been so close to tears when I hugged my parents goodbye that I thought I might cry all the way back to the city, but instead I felt a surge of excitement. I was moving forward with my plan to win back Angus's heart. All the way home I imagined the look on his face when he saw me in Kansas City. I imagined the smile that would turn up the corners of his mouth when he realized how committed I was to us. Most of all, I imagined him taking me in his arms and kissing away all the nonsense of the past several months.

Chapter 9

Charlotte

The dingy hallway smelled of burnt fish, cigarette smoke, and dirty diapers. Ironic since there was a no smoking sign only a few feet from number 1C.

Cissy, the apartment manager turned the key over and retried it. When it wouldn't even enter the keyhole, she swore under her breath and flipped it over again. "This key sticks a little, so you might have to jiggle it a few times." She wiggled the key and then pushed her bony hip into the door and tried again. Surprisingly, it clicked and Cissy stepped back to allow me to enter first.

I didn't have to go far before I knew this wasn't the apartment I'd seen online. "Um, the ad said it was fully furnished."

"Yep."

"There's not much in here."

"It's a studio," she said, like that explained the sparseness of the furnishings.

"Right. But the pictures you sent me had a bed and a small table and chairs." There had also been a coffee table, an armoire, and a dresser that had also served as an entertainment center. The photo had said the television wasn't included. Apparently, the broken down couch and the stool pushed up to the counter were the only things that were.

Cissy straightened, took a deep breath and held it for a moment as if she were willing herself not to snap. "The email said the pictures were typical of a one-bedroom apartment. You didn't ask specifically for pictures of the studio. But we don't care if you bring in more furniture. Just be sure not to muff up the walls or it'll come out of your deposit."

It took about five steps to get to the wall that made up the kitchen. I opened the door of the small refrigerator. The odor almost made me gag, and I quickly closed it. At least the light worked. I don't consider myself a snob, but I knew I'd be spending a couple of hours cleaning before I unloaded any of my belongings.

Cissy didn't seem to notice the smell. "The couch folds out, and it comes with cable TV. And you've got a parking space out there."

"I didn't see any numbers on the parking spaces, so I wasn't sure which one was mine."

"They're not numbered."

"Oh. So how do I know where I'm supposed to park?"

Cissy sighed as if the answer was obvious and I was being dim-witted on purpose. I was apparently taxing her reserve of patience. "You just park in the lot."

"There's always a spot for me?"

"Now how do you think I'm s'posed to tell you that for sure? If you get here early enough, you'll get a spot. If you don't, there's plenty of street parking."

A designated parking place was one of the things that had drawn me to the Royal Crowne apartments, so this was disappointing.

"Don't you have to pay for parking on the street?"

"Depends on where you are and what time o' day it is."

Cissy dropped the key on the counter and stepped out into the hall. "I almost forgot to tell you, Cheryl"—I didn't correct her—"you should probably leave the stick in the window. Just to be safe."

The door shut behind her, and for the first time in my life, I was living alone. I walked to the window and twisted open the blinds. On the other side of the filthy glass sat the parking lot. If I'd opened it, I could have climbed out onto the hood of a rusty, old Impala. The outside pane was cracked. An inch-thick wooden dowel barricaded the window shut. I wasn't sure if I was supposed to feel grateful that they'd provided this extra measure of security or afraid that Cissy had thought I needed it. I had hoped to be on the second or third floor, but the only available apartment not on the ground floor had been a two bedroom. I didn't need that much space, and I didn't have the money to pay for more than I needed.

I threaded the key onto my key ring, locked up, and walked out to my car. I needed to go shopping.

I dropped onto my bed after midnight. I say bed instead of couch because I'd invested in a cot and an air mattress. I couldn't imagine getting any rest on the dirty, battered couch, and although I hadn't seen any rodents since I arrived, there was something unnerving about my new home that made me want to be off the floor while I slept.

I stopped at Cissy's apartment on my way to the store and asked if the couch could be removed. I was disappointed but not surprised when she told me no and that if I did get rid of it, it would come out of my deposit. I pushed it as far into the corner as I could, covered it with a sheet, and stacked my belongings on it. For now, it would be my makeshift closet.

I had planned to go to the grocery store but I needed to clean out the cupboards and refrigerator before I filled them with food. Now that they were scrubbed and as close to sparkling as I could get them, and not one, but two boxes of baking soda were deodorizing the inside, the first order of business tomorrow would be filling them. Maybe after I got groceries, I could look at Craigslist and try to find another stool so I could invite Angus to dinner. I couldn't wait to let him know I was here. Surely the sacrifice of leaving everything behind to be with him would be enough to convince him we should be together.

Despite the late hour, I could hear the television from a neighboring apartment. I determined that the tenant liked game shows and was possibly hearing impaired. I fell asleep to the words, "Big bucks, no whammy" said over and over and over.

Glass breaking outside my window woke me up. Voices shouted and cursed and someone laughed like a hyena directly above my head. I had no idea what time it was or how long I'd been asleep. The neighbor had turned off the game shows and it was quiet except for the noise just outside my window. I snuggled deeper under my blanket, trying to calm down.

I couldn't tell how many people were on the other side of the wall. The dowel jammed into the window frame did little to settle my nerves. For the first time since I'd decided to follow Angus to Kansas City, I felt in over my head. I realized no one even knew my address here. If I disappeared, where would my family look for me?

More glass shattered against the wall. Probably a bottle. I lay there for several minutes, so tense my body began to ache.

I had wedged my phone between the cot and the air mattress. I felt around until I found it and turned it on. The screen looked too bright in the darkness, and I had the irrational thought that the voices that sounded so close could probably see the light of the screen. I pulled it under the covers and brought up my family's last group text so I could send them my address. It occurred to me that a text at this hour might cause them concern, so I quickly keyed in a message that I hoped wouldn't alarm them.

Me: Just in case I haven't given it to you, my address is

What was my address? I couldn't remember it so I deleted the message and started over.

Me: Just in case I haven't told you, my apartment is 1C in the Royal Crowne apartments. I love you all.

I tucked the phone under my pillow and tried to ignore the voices so close to my window, wishing the neighbor would wake up and have an itch to watch *Let's Make a Deal*.

I didn't sleep well the rest of the night, and I felt even more exhausted when I woke up than when I had gone to bed.

My stomach rumbled as I stepped into the shower, reminding me I needed to get groceries. I had lathered my hair when the water took a dramatic turn and became ice cold. I plastered myself against the wall, glad I'd scrubbed it. I fiddled with the faucet and finally the water returned to a comfortable temperature. I began to rinse my hair only to have it turn scalding hot.

The wall had been good enough to spare me some of the discomfort of the cold, but the fear of a blistering burn drove me out of the bathtub and I nearly fell as my feet slipped on the linoleum, water puddling around me.

I still needed to condition my hair and shave my legs. How was I going to manage an entire shower if I couldn't get more than thirty seconds of tolerable temperature?

I continued to drip on the floor as I adjusted the water. I finished my shower but I was scared and jumpy the entire time.

Cissy knocked on my door just as I was ready to leave.

"The cops was here this morning wanting to know if I heard something suspicious last night. Did they talk to you?"

"No, you're my very first visitor of the day. Or ever, come to think of it." I smiled but Cissy didn't smile back.

"I just wanted to tell you you'd best not be saying much to the cops. You don't want your neighbors to have a grudge now, do you?"

I wasn't sure how to answer that. Was it even a question?

"Well, anyway, just thought I should let you know."

What exactly had Cissy let me know? The uneasy feeling I'd had since I knocked on her apartment manager door the day before grew.

"Have a nice day," I said to Cissy's back as she started back down the dim hallway. She lifted her hand dismissively, but didn't turn around.

I stepped out into the hallway and locked my door. It smelled so bad out here. I looked along the floor for electrical sockets. There was one just under the low-wattage light fixture halfway to the front door. Should I ask Cissy if I could get a plug-in air freshener? She'd probably be offended. I'd just get one at the grocery store and plug it in. Maybe no one would notice. And maybe I'd buy a new lightbulb. Would anyone care if I changed the 25 watt bulb for something a little brighter?

I breathed in the crisp, clear air when I stepped outside. The bright sun was trying to fool us into thinking it wasn't the last week of October. Golden leaves on the trees that lined the end of the parking lot were the only clue that it was autumn.

Not too far from here—maybe just a few miles—Angus was probably doing doctorly things, completely unaware that I was so close. I felt antsy to see him. Within a few days he'd know I was here, and he'd know I meant business.

It took me a minute to realize there was a problem. I guess I'm not as observant as I'd like to think I am, because I had unlocked my car and tossed my purse into the passenger seat before I realized my car was shorter than it should be. I took a step back, looked closely, and gasped. Both tires on the driver side were flat. I stepped around to look at the other side. Sure enough, it was sitting on the rims on that side as well.

I put my hand on my forehead and staggered back a couple of steps. This wasn't an accident. I approached one of the tires, almost afraid to get too close. I ran my hand over the surface. There was a gash in the side. The gash was big enough that I doubted it could be repaired. I bit my lips. The new tires were one of the selling features when I'd found this CR-V with my parents. Now I probably had four worthless tires.

The fear I had felt when I'd heard voices in the night returned. Someone had intentionally done this to me. Maybe they were watching me right now. I glanced around but didn't see anyone acting suspiciously. Did Cissy know who had done this? Was this what she had been talking about this morning? Was she warning me not to report this? Did the noise she'd been talking about have something to do with me and my tires?

My phone rang in the car. I tried to open the passenger door to get it, but it was still locked, so I hurried around to reach through the car for it.

It was Will.

"Hey, Sis. How's it going?"

I would have answered him, but I couldn't. My throat had completely closed off, and forming words was impossible. In fact, breathing had become difficult. I tried to drag in a breath but it took a moment, and when I finally pulled in enough air to survive, it escaped again in an ugly sob.

"Charles, what's going on?" Will sounded scared, and I somehow needed to let him know I was okay.

"Just . . . Oh . . . It's . . ."

"Charles, say something. Are you hurt?"

I dropped down onto the curb by the car. "Will. I'm not hurt, but . . . It's just that . . ." I tried to think of something to tell him that wouldn't worry him. If I told him what had happened to my car, and how awful my apartment was, and about the voices right outside my window . . . Dad and Mom would be on the first flight out and they'd insist on moving me back home.

"Don't try to sugarcoat it, Chuck. I can tell you're about to. You'd better tell me the truth."

I sighed. "Okay, but only if you promise not to tell Mom and Dad."

"You know I can't promise that. Not if something's really wrong."

"Please don't tell them. I'll be fine, and I have to be here."

"Just tell me what's happening."

And so I told him. Everything. He didn't interrupt me, but I could sense through the phone, even across two thousand miles, that Will was fuming.

"You need to turn this in to your insurance. They'll probably help pay for tires. But you've got to call the police first. The insurance company will want a police report."

"I'm not sure if I should do that."

"Do what?"

"Call the police."

"Of course you should. That's vandalism and destruction of property."

"But . . ."

"Charlotte, there are no buts. Call the police."

"The landlady kind of told me not to."

"What?" I had thought Will was angry before, but now I could practically smell the smoke coming out of his ears. He was a prosecutor, after all. He was probably seeing every intimidated witness he'd ever heard of flashing before his eyes.

"Charles, go in your apartment."

"Why?"

"Lock up your car, go in your apartment, and wait until you hear from me."

"What are you going to do? Are you going to call the police? Don't call the police." I don't know why skin-and-bone Cissy had me intimidated, but I figured she'd been sent to warn me by other people, people who probably weren't skin and bone.

"I'm going to have your car towed someplace that can fix your tires. Go in your apartment until they get there."

Will's intensity was making my blood pressure rise.

"You're at the Royal Crowne apartments, right?"

"You got my message?"

Will's laugh sounded a little like a bark. "Yeah. I got it. Is your car locked?"

I picked up my purse and then locked the door. "It

69

is now."

"Are you in your apartment?"

"I'm not that fast. But I'm on my way."

"Tell me when you're inside with the door locked."

I made my way down the dark hall. I must have been upset because I hardly noticed the sour smell. "I'm in."

"Is the door locked?"

"Yes."

"Just wait there. I'll call AAA. We need to get your car working, and then we'll talk about what you need to do to move."

"I don't think I can afford to move."

"Well, you can't stay there."

I sat down on the one stool at the counter. It shifted under me, feeling loose-jointed and risky. Worried I might break it and lose my deposit, I moved a suitcase off the couch and sat down on the sheet. I looked around my seedy, light-deprived apartment (I'd need to invest in some higher-wattage light bulbs for in here, too) and surveyed my situation. I was alone in a large, unfamiliar city. I'd be completely unemployed as soon as I finished the two projects Jayne had encouraged me to bring with me. I lived in a dump. And I was the victim of a crime that I'd been warned not to report.

My eyes settled on the stool I'd been sitting on. It tilted a little to the left, and I could see that if I'd stayed there, I'd certainly have ended up on the floor.

And then I laughed. If this didn't show Angus I was willing to do almost anything to win back his heart, nothing would.

Chapter 10

Angus

The car in front of me slowed down before the light even turned yellow.

"Come on, you can make that." I pounded my fist on the steering wheel and came to a stop behind the overly cautious driver. I picked up my phone and looked at the address again. Had Charles completely lost her mind? Even though I was new to Kansas City, I could have told her to steer clear of this part of town. She should have asked me.

I flinched a little at that thought, knowing I hadn't made it easy for her to call me. But wasn't that the point? The lack of communication should have been enough to make it clear that Charlotte shouldn't be here. She should be in San Francisco, moving on with her life. Instead, she was here by herself in a dangerous part of a city she knew nothing about.

I won't lie. When Will had called and told me Charlotte was here, my shock had quickly morphed to thrill. Had she really followed me all this way? Had she given up her dream job and moved away from her family for me? For so many years a move like that would have been just what I wanted. It didn't take long before the thrill I felt over Charles following me turned into alarm.

Charlotte could be so maddening, but I wasn't only frustrated with her. I was also frustrated with myself. I didn't want to be happy she had come. I didn't even want to see her. She had a way of tearing down my resolve, and I couldn't let her do it this time.

I wouldn't let her do it this time. I would send her home. I didn't have time for Charlotte to be here. I needed to be focused right now. Combining my residency with the fellowship meant long hours and hard work. There wasn't time to date and play around and take care of a girlfriend.

I passed the careful driver as soon as we pulled through the intersection. It was an ancient woman who could barely see over the steering wheel. She reminded me of my grandma, and I felt guilty for my impatience.

My phone rang in my hand. It was Will.

"Hey man, I'm already on my way."

"Good. The tow truck will be there within the hour. I'm not dragging you away from anything important, I hope."

"Not unless you think sleep or getting groceries is important."

"I was afraid you'd be at work."

"For once Chuck's timing is good. This is the first day I've had off in the last eight. I go back tomorrow for another four days straight, so if she was going to pick a time to need rescuing, she picked the right day."

Will must not have liked my sarcastic tone because he was quiet. "Be nice to her, Angus. She's sacrificed a lot to come out there and show you how much she cares."

I gritted my teeth and measured my words. "Yeah, well I didn't ask her to come. I don't want her here. I needed some separation so I can get on with my life." I sighed. "And I've got way too much on my plate without having to worry Charlotte is okay."

Will groaned. "You know, Angus. You two deserve each other. I used to think Charles was the blind one, but now I can see you're both clueless and stupid and stubborn."

"I don't think . . ."

"Exactly." Will's voice was hard as he interrupted me. "Neither of you think. You've both spent years letting everything happen to you instead of thinking things through and then taking matters into your own hands."

"I tried. Over and over."

"Angus?" Will's voice was stern. "You need to stop playing the victim. Sure, Charlotte might have been clueless, but it's time for you to take responsibility for your own part in this mess. You were always too afraid to speak up and tell her how you felt. You expected her to read your mind. Maybe she should have, but you're not blameless."

There was a long pause. I wanted to stick up for myself, to remind Will how long I'd been waiting on her, but I was worn out. Not only was I sleep deprived, I was tired of analyzing the whole Charlotte situation. That was one of the reasons I'd left San Francisco. I was exhausted. So rather than argue, I let the silence stretch out between us until finally Will spoke again.

"Look, I don't know how you two are going to work through all this, but if you're too proud to accept what she's trying to do, at least let her down easy. Remember that you used to be friends and treat her that way."

It was an irrational reaction, but suddenly I felt betrayed

by Will. Of course he was worried about how I was going to treat Charlotte. But what about how Charlotte had treated me? I'd never have expected him to turn his back on his sister, but was it too much to ask that he try to look at both sides? Did he have to make it so obvious whose side he was on now?

"Look Will, I'm on my way over there to get her. I'll make sure she's safe and I'll send her back home. Then you can figure out a way to keep her there. You shouldn't have let her come."

"I couldn't have stopped her even if I'd thought she was making a huge mistake. And I didn't, by the way. I thought it was the right thing for her to do. And brave too. But whatever." Will was clearly annoyed. "I've got to go. Text me when you're with her."

Will hung up before I could answer. He was furious, and it made me even more irritated with Chuck.

The Royal Crowne had been a beautiful building a hundred years ago. It still looked impressive from far away, but on closer inspection, you could see the wood rotting under the eaves and around the windows. I didn't see Charlotte's Bug, but when I saw California plates on a CRV with four flats, I realized she had a different car.

Charlotte had loved that little car. I felt a twinge of something I didn't want to analyze.

Charlotte's car wasn't the only undriveable one in the lot, but the two others sporting flat tires looked like they'd been sitting there since the turn of the century.

I swear something had died in the hallway. Maybe it was still there, but how would we know. It was the middle of the day, and the hallway was almost dark.

I heard some movement inside 1C when I knocked.

"Who is it?"

The sound of her voice on the other side of the door did

74

something to me. I knew her well enough to hear the uncertainty she was trying to cover with a show of confidence. I wasn't ready to face the girl I had hoped not to see until my heart had healed.

I rested my hand on the top of the doorframe and buried my face against my sleeve, blocking the stench and bracing myself to see her.

"Is someone there?"

"It's me, Charles."

She fumbled with the locks and swung the door open. She looked so excited to see me that I nearly let her hug me, which would probably have been a mistake.

I stepped past her and into the tiny room. It was an awful place.

Boxes and suitcases sat on a couch in the corner and a cot was made up under the window. I turned back toward her. "Charles, what are you doing?"

"I was heading out to get groceries, but someone slashed my tires."

"You know that's not what I mean." I tried to keep the frustration out of my voice.

It took her a minute to answer, like she was choosing her words carefully or trying not to cry. "Can we talk about this later? I need to get my tires fixed."

"You need to do more than get your tires fixed. You can't live here, Chuck. This isn't a safe area."

"I didn't know." Her voice was almost a whisper.

She sounded defeated, and the old Angus—the one who had loved Charlotte forever—wanted to comfort her, but I kept several feet between us. The sidewalk in front of her San Francisco apartment had proven I had no willpower when it came to Charlotte.

"There's a tow truck coming. They'll be here any minute. Let's get your stuff loaded in my car."

"But I've paid the rent here. And a deposit."

"It doesn't matter. You're not staying here. Will threatened my life if I don't have you out of here before noon." I looked at my watch. It was nearly one o'clock.

"You're still safe if we go by Pacific Time." Her smile was weak, but I was glad to see a little of her humor. I smiled back.

"Then we'd better get started."

We had carried most of her things to my car when the tow truck arrived.

"Looks like you've got an enemy," the wiry driver said, an unlit cigarette bouncing between his lips as he talked.

"I don't know anyone here, so I'm not sure how I managed to make an enemy already." Charlotte looked agitated.

"You reported this, right?" the man asked.

Charlotte shook her head.

"You should do that before I move the car."

She shook her head again. "That's okay. I just want to get it fixed."

"Are you sure, Charles? It wouldn't take long to get someone here."

"I'm sure. Please, just take it."

We both stared at her for a few extra seconds and then the driver looked at me. I shrugged and he kept working.

When the truck left, carrying Charlotte's crippled car on a trailer, we loaded the last few things into my car.

"You should lock up and turn in your key. I'll come with you."

I stood a little behind Charlotte. She knocked twice before the landlady answered the door. Her clothes hung limply on her lanky body, like she'd lost some weight but had never replaced her wardrobe. She folded her arms tightly and glanced warily at me while Charles asked for a refund.

"Who's he?" She inclined her head my direction.

"He's my friend."

"He's not a cop?"

Charlotte shook her head.

The landlady glared at me a couple of seconds before she said, "Sorry. It's not refundable." She didn't sound sorry.

I took a step forward, and the landlady bristled. "Her car was damaged here last night. It's not a safe apartment. You should let her have her money back and you can rent it to someone else."

"She shoulda read her contract."

"Ma'am." Charlotte smiled. "You requested that I not call the police, and I haven't. Maybe, as a goodwill gesture, you could give me a refund. Even if it's just the deposit."

This made me angry. If I had known Charlotte wasn't calling the police because this woman had warned her off, I'd have called them myself.

"Call the police. You've moved the car out of the parking lot. There's no way to prove anything even happened here."

"Maybe we should call them." I took my phone out of my pocket.

"Go ahead." The woman lifted her chin a little. She seemed pretty sure of herself.

Charlotte handed the key to the woman and took my arm, pulling me toward the door. "Let's go." I resisted at first, but then her voice became pleading. "Please, Angus. Let's get out of here."

I let her lead me out to the parking lot. Three guys passed us just outside the door, one of them bumping me hard with his shoulder.

He stopped and turned toward us. His eyes never left Charles as we walked to the car, and I felt a cold dread settle over me when I thought about her spending the night here alone. Charlotte had to go home. I had to convince her she shouldn't be here. She needed to go back to her job, and her family, and especially her safe neighborhood.

Charles got in the car and closed the door. I met and held his eyes over my open door, determined to let him know that Charlotte wasn't alone.

"Come on, Angus." Her voice sounded panicky, so I got in and we left. The man on the step watched us until the building blocked his view.

Charles stared out the window as we drove across the city. The car was uncomfortably quiet, but I wasn't sure what to say. I didn't want to offer words of encouragement and give her the wrong idea, but now wasn't the time to tell her how foolish she'd been.

We were almost to my apartment when she finally spoke. "I don't have anywhere to go."

"I know. Hopefully they can have your car fixed by tomorrow, and you can head back home." Charles looked like I'd slapped her, and I felt terrible. "Please don't feel bad. It's just that you should have talked to me before you came."

"You'd have told me not to come."

What could I say? She was right.

I pulled into the parking lot of the Milton Apartments and into my assigned parking spot. "What do you need for one night?"

"You can take me to a hotel."

"You can stay here. I'm headed back to the hospital this evening." I wasn't scheduled to work again until tomorrow morning, but there was a break room with a futon, and it would be easier to sleep there than to spend a night in an

78

apartment with a girl I'd loved and was trying to put behind me. "I'm not sure you can afford a hotel, anyway. Stay here tonight and call Jayne. See if you can get your job back."

Charles didn't say anything, and I could tell by her expression she was digging her heels in. Arguing with her wouldn't get us anywhere.

"What do you need for tonight?"

Chuck relaxed a little and pointed to a suitcase. "Just that one."

I carried her bag up one flight of stairs and into my small, one-bedroom apartment. The contrast between this cozy, clean apartment and the place we'd just left was stark.

Charlotte looked around. "What are you paying for this? If you don't mind me asking."

I tried not to smile, but failed a little. "More than you were paying. Unless you count replacing four tires as part of your rent."

"Ha ha. You don't want to tell me, do you?"

"I'd tell you, but I don't want to encourage this irrational behavior. You need to go home." He turned and walked into the bedroom. "I don't know what you were thinking." I was talking to myself with that last sentence, but of course she heard me.

"You know exactly what I was thinking." She spoke under her breath, and I decided it was best not to say anything back.

Chapter 11

Charlotte

*A*ngus's apartment was nice—a little small, but after the pit I'd lived in for a day, it looked luxurious. I felt sick that I'd lost a significant amount of money to Cissy and was about to lose even more to Sid's Garage, but what was I to do? I could mope and cry about how badly things were going, or I could look forward and press on with my mission. It didn't matter what Angus said. It would take a lot more than this to make me give up and go back to San Francisco.

My stomach quietly snarled, reminding me that it was afternoon, and I still hadn't had a bite to eat.

"Hey, Angus? Do you have any food?"

Angus stuck his head around the corner. "You haven't eaten anything, have you?"

I shook my head.

"Oh, Chuck." His voice was sympathetic and tugged at my heart. "I don't have much. I was about to go get groceries when Will called."

"Me too. I mean, I was on my way to the grocery store when I found my tires slashed. What if my car had been fine? Maybe we would have run into each other in the produce section."

"Probably not. I would have been in a reputable store and in the freezer section. I rarely have time for anything more than a sandwich or a frozen meal. When I first got here, I bought a bunch of fruit and vegetables and then I worked a week straight. Most of it went bad."

Angus went into the kitchen and pulled out a bread bag. "There are two crusts. You want them?"

"What about you?"

"I had breakfast."

"Do you have any peanut butter?"

"I do. And I even have a little jam. Your favorite." He pulled a nearly empty jar of blackberry jam out of the refrigerator. "Sit down." With the knife in his hand, he motioned toward a sturdy-looking barstool pushed up to the counter. I sat and watched him make the sandwich. "Sorry. No milk." He slid a glass of water to me and pulled out the stool next to mine. He scooted it several inches from me and sat down.

"What would you have thought if we had run into each other at the store?" I asked.

Angus shook his head. "I'd have thought you had a twin because you're much too smart to do something this nuts."

"A twin, huh? You know me having a twin isn't that far-fetched."

Angus laughed. "I guess I'd have thought you and Will had a long lost triplet."

"Would you have introduced yourself to this look-alike?"

"Hmm." Angus's face turned serious.

"Wouldn't you want to be the hero that reunited her with her true family?"

"Probably not. I think I'd have headed for the exit."

"Wow. Some hero you are."

"Yeah, well, if she looked like you, introducing myself would be counter-productive since I moved out here to forget about you."

"Oh."

Suddenly the conversation felt like I was perched on a mountain of Jell-O. One word could send me slipping and sliding down the slope until there would be no way to get back. I took the last bites of my sandwich in silence, and when I finished, Angus put the plate and glass in the sink and cleared his throat.

"Speaking of grocery stores, I have to go or I'll spend the next week with nothing to eat. Do you need anything?"

"Can I come with you?" I held my breath, praying he wouldn't reject me.

"Go ahead. I'm not your boss."

Those were wonderful words, and they melted all the slippery Jell-O away. I can't remember who had said that phrase first, but Angus, Will, and I had said it many times over the years. When two of us were involved in a game and the third asked to join, one or both of us would say, "Go ahead. I'm not your boss." If someone was going somewhere and the others asked to tag along, the answer was, "If you want to. I'm not your boss." I'm not sure if it was the sentimental phrase or the thought of walking down the aisles of the grocery store that made me silly with happiness.

"We can get you some Lorna Doones and some Pringles."

Ouch! He really knew how to hurt a girl. I love Lorna Doones and Pringles, but years ago, I had decided I would only allow myself those unhealthy snacks when I was road tripping. Angus's suggestion plainly told me he planned on me being California bound, junk food in tow, as soon as possible.

"Man, you really want me out of here." I tried to keep it light and was glad that he played along.

"Nothing to see here. Move along." He softened the words with a smile, and I decided I'd save the news that I wasn't going anywhere for another time.

At the grocery store, I pretended I didn't notice when Angus put the cookies and chips in the cart. They wouldn't be eaten on a road trip. I vowed I wouldn't touch one cookie or eat one chip. He'd have to eat them himself or let them grow stale in his kitchen cabinet. I added a package of lasagna noodles and Angus gave me a questioning look.

"For chicken lasagna. I thought we could have some tonight, before you leave for the hospital."

"You don't have to cook for me, Chuck."

"I know. But it's the least I can do to thank you for rescuing me today."

"You don't have to thank me."

"Yeah, I do."

"No, you don't. Friends help each other."

"Well this friend"—I emphasized the word friend—"is fixing you dinner tonight."

"I guess it can be a farewell dinner before that friend"—he pointed at me—"leaves town tomorrow."

I rolled my eyes and started for the meat department, pulling the cart, and Angus, along behind me.

Angus purchased a few easy-to-prepare things for the coming week, and we returned to his apartment.

"Do you mind putting the groceries away?" he asked after

setting the bags on the counter. "I've got a couple of errands I need to run, and I've got to get some laundry started in the basement on my way out."

"Aren't you worried someone will steal it?"

Angus smiled. "This isn't The Royal Crowne. And I've got a key. Only residents can get in there, and I haven't had a problem yet."

My imagination got a little ahead of itself while I put away the groceries and started dinner. I tried to close the door on the eager thoughts, but like sunshine that teases through the clouds, suggesting maybe it will warm up enough for an afternoon picnic, wishful thoughts kept peeking around the corners of my mind. *If all goes well, this will be your life. You'll be in a cute, little apartment, fixing Angus dinner. Someday, he'll walk through that door and be happy to see you. He'll tell you how nice it is to come home to you and a delicious dinner instead of to a lonely, empty apartment. He'll let out a long, satisfied sigh and walk straight to the kitchen, where he'll put his arms around you and kiss you. Sometimes it will be a kiss that takes your breath away, because he's missed you and you belong to each other and he can't get enough of you. Other times it will be a kiss on the forehead, just because he likes you so much. Then, once in a while, he'll kiss the end of your nose, because he's in a playful mood and you've said something clever.*

I couldn't decide if letting my imagination take me that far down the road was a good thing or a bad one. I could argue the case that it was good to visualize the end goal, but I also knew that if Angus didn't have a change of heart, all my visualizing would make it that much harder to lose him for good. Still, I couldn't help but long for that warm, affectionate homecoming.

The Wife maker

Chapter 12

Charlotte

*I*t was almost midnight when the phone rang. I was still up. Angus had told me to sleep in his bed since he'd be at the hospital and had even changed the sheets before he left, but I had been too busy looking up apartments and job postings to go to bed.

The screen showed a picture of Will holding Emily above his head while she giggled. It made me smile and long to play with my sweet niece.

"Hi, Will."

"Where are you?"

"What? No pleasantries or small talk?"

"Sorry. I was in meetings until about an hour ago, and I've worried about you all day. I wanted to be sure you're okay."

"I'm fine."

"Please tell me you're not at that apartment you rented.

Angus said it was terrible."

"Yeah. It was. What were your meetings about?" I was tired of being the topic of conversation.

"The Devlin case starts tomorrow. We met all day with the defense, hoping for a last-minute deal, but they're having none of it. Ineffective counsel if you ask me. They should be jumping at our offer. He's going to end up in prison for twenty years because of their bad advice."

"That should make you happy, shouldn't it? You said he's guilty."

"He is, but that doesn't mean I want him to have lousy representation. Our offer was fair. I think his lawyer wants the publicity he's going to get from such a high-profile case. He's in it for himself instead of his client. So tomorrow we start jury selection. We spent all evening meeting with our jury consultants."

"You've been so busy with this. Sorry I worried you."

"Yeah, not cool, Chuck. I get that you were anxious to go make amends with Angus, but I thought you were smarter than to go off halfcocked. Please tell me you called the police about your tires." Will groaned when I didn't answer. "You're making me regret that I came in on your side with the family, Charles."

"Please tell me you haven't told Mom and Dad."

"Not yet."

"Not ever, Will. I don't want them to worry about me."

"They're already worried. And if they knew about this, they'd know their worries are justified. If you're going to do grown up things like move and change jobs, you need to be smart. Why didn't you call the police?"

"I just wanted out of there."

"You're a disgrace to my profession." There was no more

edge to his voice and I was happy to hear him crack a joke.

"You're the prosecutor, not me. I just wanted out of there without having to deal with Cissy, or anyone else, once I was gone."

"Says every intimidated witness. You haven't answered me. Where are you?"

"I'm at Angus's. He's at the hospital. He said I could stay here tonight, but he wants me on the road tomorrow morning as soon as my tires are fixed."

"He said that?"

"More than once."

Will's voice sounded sympathetic. "Sorry, Charles. That's probably not the outcome you were hoping for."

Will's sympathy was like a cord tightening around my throat, and I knew I was dangerously close to crying. That would really show him I was behaving like a responsible adult.

"No. Not what I pictured."

"How were you planning on letting him know you were there?"

"I thought I'd get settled, and in a day or two, I'd invite him to dinner. He'd find out when I gave him the address. And he'd be so thrilled I was here that everything would be better."

"Nice thought, but I'm afraid he's not going to be that easily convinced."

"Believe me, I know. Reality has punched me in the face a few times in the last twenty-four hours."

"Are you okay?"

I laughed as a couple of tears escaped my eyes.

"Sure."

"Seriously, Chuck. Are you?"

I sniffed and wiped my eyes on my sleeve.

"I will be. If Angus thinks I came all this way to fail,

he's wrong. I'm not leaving."

"That's fine, but only if you find a safe place to live."

"I've been looking online ever since Angus left."

"Didn't you find your last place online?"

"Don't worry. I'm reading reviews, and I'll ask more questions. And I'm here now, so I can check them out in person."

"Be careful."

"I will. Thanks for calling Angus and sending him to help me."

"Yeah. What exactly were your plans before I called?"

"I don't know. I'd just found the tires, so I hadn't had a chance to think about what to do. I couldn't believe they were all flat."

"It must have been scary."

"It was. The whole place was kinda terrifying. I don't know if I'd have had the guts to stay there another night."

"That wouldn't have shown guts. It would have shown lack of judgment. Just be more careful. Please."

"I will." I told him to give Gina and Emily a hug, and we said goodbye. Suddenly I felt exhausted. I closed the laptop and got ready for bed.

There was a soft knock at the front door of the apartment right before it opened.

"It's me," Angus said before he rounded the corner. "I didn't want to startle you."

"Hi. I didn't know if I'd see you today."

It had been a productive day but I wasn't sure if Angus

would be happy about what I had accomplished.

"I called the shop and they told me your car had been ready since this morning, but that you hadn't come to get it. I figured I could run you over during my dinner break."

"Thank you. I was about to call a cab to take me over before they close."

"I was surprised you hadn't picked it up. I thought you might already be on your way home."

I frowned. I had been too busy to think much about it. I had called on several apartments before I convinced myself it would be okay to check at the office here in Angus's complex. I had rejected that idea at first, knowing how unhappy Angus would be about it, but the more I thought about it, the more it seemed like a good idea. The least I could do is check.

I had spoken to Daphne, an older lady with short, curly hair that fell across one eye.

"We have a one-bedroom unit that's empty, but the tenants had a dog in there. You don't have a dog, do you?"

I shook my head. "No, no pets."

"Good. We don't allow dogs, but it smells like they had three or four of them. The carpet was just plain sick. Of course, they lost their deposit. Anyway, the new carpet won't be laid until Saturday. I'm having my son-in-law install it, and he didn't have time until the weekend. But after that, you could rent it. It's number 213. I'll let you take it for the same price as the last folks since I won't have to advertise it. But only if you promise not to have a dog in there. Or any pet. I don't even want a fish in there. A few years ago, some renters begged and begged to have a fish tank for their little girl. Supposed to help her learn some responsibility. Um hmm. I'll be danged if that thing didn't spring a leak and warp the floor under it. So now we have a policy. No pets at all."

"No pets here." I smiled and put my hands up

in surrender.

Daphne smiled back.

"And that unit's furnished?" I was hoping it would look as nice as Angus's apartment.

Daphne opened a folder and flipped through a couple of papers. "This one has the basics. Nothing too fancy. But the bed's pretty new."

By the time I paid the rent and the required deposit, I was panicking. Once I deducted the car repairs from my account, I'd have less than two hundred dollars in the bank. I hadn't been this depleted on funds since I was in college. I had a check coming from Jayne next week and another one as soon as I turned in my last project, but I needed to find work here. I wouldn't last long if I didn't.

I had nearly sprinted back to Angus's apartment so I could look for work. There were no jobs available that made me excited. In fact, the job situation was dismal. Would I ever find something I'd enjoy as much as my job at Jayne Fife? I felt a little encouraged by the fact that there were temporary, seasonal jobs being posted. If all else failed, I could wrap Christmas presents at a department store.

"Do you want me to warm up some lasagna for you?" If Angus was using his dinner break to take me to pick up my car, I didn't want him to go hungry.

"Nah, let's go get your car and see if there's time to eat when we get back."

Angus was quiet as we drove to the garage, and I could tell he had something on his mind.

"How was work today?"

"Busy."

After a few more blocks of silence, I tried again.

"Is everything okay?"

He raised his eyebrows and looked at me sideways. "Just a lot on my mind." His tone let me know he didn't want to talk, so I didn't push him.

It didn't take long to get my car. There had been an extra charge for balancing the tires that hadn't initially been quoted, and I swallowed hard as I watched my bank account sputter and choke.

"Ya'll come back now," said an old guy who might have been Sid. I smiled and waved, whole-heartedly hoping I wouldn't have a need to come see Sid again.

I followed Angus back to his apartment and pulled my car into a visitor parking place. I could have pulled into my own, newly-assigned spot, but I wasn't ready to inform Angus that he now had a new neighbor.

Back in his apartment, I dished up two plates of food and put one in the microwave. Angus leaned against the counter, his legs stretched out in front of him, and his arms folded. "You should stay here again tonight and head out tomorrow morning. It's not a good idea to be driving by yourself late at night."

I turned my back to him and switched the plates in the microwave. I could tell he was waiting for a response, but I didn't want to argue with him.

"Did you hear me?" Angus asked.

"Yeah."

"We should have topped off your gas tank on the way home so you'd be ready to roll in the morning."

"You should eat." I motioned to the plate of steaming food. Angus pushed off the counter and sat down to eat.

"Do you know how much gas you have?"

I had about half a tank, but that didn't matter. I took a glass out of the cupboard, filled it with ice and water and placed it in front of him.

"Chuck? Are you purposely ignoring me?"

I shook my head. "No. I heard you."

"Do you know how much gas is in your tank?"

"I've got enough."

Angus looked up from his plate and studied me. He didn't look happy.

"Enough?" His voice was steely.

I stood across the counter from him and met his eyes. "Angus, I'm not going home."

"Yes, you are."

I shook my head. "I'm not. I found an apartment today, and I have some jobs I'll be checking on tomorrow."

Angus put down his fork and laced his fingers together in front of him, stretching his fingers back, first on one hand and then the other as he thought. He took a deep breath. "Charlotte, why did you come here?"

Maybe if I was honest, he wouldn't be so determined to send me away? "For you."

"That's a nice thought, and I appreciate it. Really, I do. But you need to listen to me. This isn't happening." He unclasped his hands and motioned between us. "We're not happening. You don't belong here and you need to go home."

I swallowed hard. No matter how disappointed I was, I would not cry. Even though nothing had gone according to plan, I would stay focused and determined. Will and Flynn both thought it would take a grand gesture, and perhaps the grandest gesture of all would be not giving up too easily.

I squared my shoulders and looked Angus in the eye. "I'm not leaving. I came here because I miss you. I want to be where you are. If you want me to go back to San Francisco, I will. But you'll have to come, too."

"You know I can't go back. I have to be here."

"Then so do I." I made my voice as firm and determined as I could muster. Angus took several long, slow breaths, and I knew he was trying to figure out what to say that would convince me to go back to San Francisco. I continued, my voice pleading. "I'm sorry it took me so long to get a clue. I'm sorry I hurt you."

Angus laughed a bitter laugh but didn't interrupt me.

"Angus, I want to make things right. You're my best friend. I love you, and I think you still love me, too. Stop being so stubborn and accept my apology." Angus rubbed his hands over his face, and I added, "I'm not going back home. I'm staying here. With you."

"There's no point in you being here. I don't have time for anything but work. You're lucky you needed rescuing yesterday. Most days I couldn't have come."

"I won't need to be rescued again."

When Angus finally spoke, his voice was slow and measured. "I accept your apology, Charles. All's forgiven. You don't need to feel bad anymore." He stood and slowly pushed the stool up to the counter, his meal almost untouched. "The thing is, I think I was mistaking my feelings of sympathy with feelings of love. I always felt so bad for you. I always wanted to fix things." Every word was like a blow. A smart fighter would go down for the count and save themselves the bruises.

He must have known he was about to deliver a knockout punch because he walked to the door, and with his back to me, he said the words that were meant to level me. "Charlotte, I don't want you here."

He closed the door behind him without looking back.

And that was his mistake. If he wanted me to leave, he'd have to look me in the eyes and tell me.

Chapter 13

Charlotte

A ngus was avoiding me. I texted him to see if I could stay at his apartment for a few days since mine wouldn't be ready until Monday, and he grudgingly agreed. At first I took that as a good sign. At least I would see him when he came home to shower and change. But I was wrong. When he came home on Thursday, it was for less than an hour, and when he left, he was carrying a small suitcase.

"I have a key, so when you leave on Monday, you can leave yours on the counter."

"You don't have to leave because of me, Angus. I can stay at a hotel."

"It's fine. It's just until Monday."

I didn't see or hear from him again for almost a week. I moved my few things into apartment 213. My apartment was in a different building than Angus's, but I could see his parking spot from mine and his front door from my bedroom window. His car was almost always gone. He was off being a doctor and learning about hips.

I, on the other hand, had too much time on my hands. I finished my last souvenir project for Jayne—a set of four prints for t-shirts for a whitewater rafting company in Wyoming. I had mixed feelings when I sent off the prints. Sad because I'd miss working for Jayne. Apprehension because I didn't have a replacement job yet. Elation because I really needed that last check.

And now I was officially unemployed. I had sent my resume to several companies, including Hallmark. They sent me a pleasant response telling me they were impressed with my experience, but they weren't hiring. So far the only company that had invited me in for an interview was a temporary staffing agency. I was meeting with Mark this afternoon.

My phone played "Copacabana" and I braced myself to take Mom's call.

It had been two weeks since I'd left San Francisco. So far I'd done most of the calling between us. I needed to control the narrative and that was much easier if I made the phone calls. I had told her about Angus saving the day. She liked the sound of that. I didn't tell her about his rebuff. I had told her about my second apartment. She wanted to know what it looked like, so I texted her pictures. They put her mind at ease. She wanted to know about jobs, so I had told her I had an interview today. That was probably what she was calling about.

"Hi, Mom," I said as I applied mascara.

"Charlotte. How are you?"

"I'm great. Just getting ready for a job interview this afternoon." I should give myself a good poke in the eye with my mascara wand for lying to my mom like this. I wasn't doing great. I was broke and lonely and Angus didn't want me here.

"Yes, I wanted to wish you luck. What company is it?"

"It's called CRS. Creative Resource Solutions."

"Sounds like a perfect fit."

I held the phone between my ear and shoulder and closed the mascara. "It does?"

"Yes. You're one of the most creative people I know." I breathed a sigh of relief, glad the founder of the company had chosen a name that wouldn't immediately let my parents know I was applying to be a temp.

"Thanks, Mom."

"You'll do great. I'm sure they'll be impressed with your portfolio."

I smiled. They didn't even want to see my portfolio. Their creativity didn't mean artistic ability. It meant they'd send a graphic artist to wait tables or an engineer to chop carrots. But Mom didn't need to know that.

"How's Angus?"

"He's great. Really busy. He puts in a lot of hours."

"Be sure to tell him hi for us, okay?"

"I will. For sure. I'll tell him the next time I see him. I'm sure he says hi back."

"We miss you, honey, but I have to say I'm proud of you. I hope Angus knows how lucky he is."

"I'm sure he does." I cringed as I wound myself tighter and tighter in my web of deceit. "I've got to go, Mom. Please give Dad a hug and tell everyone hello."

"I will, Charlotte. I love you."

I hung up feeling a little sick. I needed Angus to come around so I could honestly tell my family everything was going well.

Mark was like Anderson Cooper on amphetamines. He was handsome, in a graying, middle-aged man sort of way. He talked so fast it was hard to keep up, but I soon realized that he made up for his rapid-fire speech by repeating most things at least once.

"What kind of work are you hoping for?" he asked.

"I've been designing souvenirs, but I can certainly do other kinds of graphic design."

"Of course, you can. Of course, you can. This says you have no criminal history?"

"No. I got a speeding ticket once, but . . ."

"That's not criminal. Not criminal at all. We drug test around here. Will drug testing be a problem for you?"

"No."

Mark looked up from his computer and looked me over again. "No, I didn't think so. I didn't think so. If we don't immediately have something that uses your artistic skills, are you interested in being placed in other positions? Temporarily, of course." He laughed. "We are a temp agency, after all, so most of our positions are temporary, but just in case we don't have something that uses your skills, we'd like to be able to send you out on other positions."

"I really need a job, so I'm open to other things. As long as they're legal." I smiled at my little joke, but Mark looked at me seriously.

"Of course our jobs are legal. Why would we care if you have a criminal record if we're going to send you out on an illegal job?"

I laughed nervously. "Oh, you wouldn't. I was just joking."

Mark smiled. "Ah, I get it. I get it." He laughed and nodded his head. "I get it." He turned back to the computer screen in front of him. "How soon can you start?"

I would have said, "Yesterday," but I wasn't sure now if he would appreciate my sarcasm, so I opted for, "Tomorrow."

He scrolled through some pages on his computer. "Tomorrow. What do we have tomorrow? Plumber's assistant? No. Drywaller? No. Driver?" He looked at me. "No. Sous chef? Sous chef. At Escape in the Marriott. Hmm. Any experience in the kitchen? I don't mean classically trained chef, I just mean do you have any experience cooking."

"I cook at home."

He ran his finger along his computer screen as he read. "Food prep, general kitchen help and cleanup." He turned to me. "Think you can do that? We can send you out tomorrow if you can do that." He looked back at the listing. "Ah, and it's a position that lasts two weeks. If they like you, that is. That's the beauty of our industry. If you don't like each other, there's no obligation to keep you. Of course, we want them to keep you. Yes, yes. We want them to be happy with you. And we'll be more inclined to send you out on future jobs if past employers have liked you. Yes, it's important they like you."

"I'll definitely do my best." I wanted to wrap up this conversation. Mark was giving me a headache.

I filled out the necessary papers and left the offices of Creative Resource Solutions with a smile on my face. Things were looking up. I had a job. For at least two weeks. Unless they didn't like me. My smile faltered only a little.

I hadn't seen Angus since the day he'd taken a suitcase to the hospital, but when I pulled into the Milton parking lot after my job interview, his car was in its spot. I considered walking to his apartment and telling him my good news, but I was happy about this sous chef job and I didn't want to see a look of disappointment on Angus's face when I told him about it. I texted him instead. Given the long, drawn-out and depressing nature of our texts the last few months, I decided to spill it all in one long text. It ended up going through as three separate texts with awkward breaks, but once I'd hit the send button, there was nothing I could do about it anyway.

Me: You've been a busy man. I didn't mean to kick you out of your apartment. I felt terrible that you felt you couldn't be there while I was there. I should have just gotten a hotel so I wouldn't interrupt your life too much. But I'm grateful for the place to stay until my apartment was available. I don't think I ever told you where I'm living now. You were in a hurry to leave that day and I didn't want to make you angry. I still don't want to make you angry, but since you're the only person I know here in Kansas City (except a couple of apartment managers and a temporary employment manager), I kinda want you to know where I am. I'm living in a nice complex not too far from you. You've probably heard of them. They're the Milton Apartments. Yes, you guessed it. I'm living in the same complex as you. I live in the D Building, number 213. We're neighbors!

We haven't lived this close since we were kids. In fact, I think this might be even closer, but that's beside the point.

Me: I got a job today. Sort of. I mean, it is a job, but it's not permanent. I'm starting tomorrow at the Marriott. I'm going to be a sous chef at Escape. The job lasts two weeks. Then who knows what I'll be doing. That's the beauty of temp work, right? Nothing is too predictable. Actually, I hope the temp work is only temporary. :) I'd really like to work at

Hallmark, but they don't have any openings right now. I'll have to keep checking back and keep my eyes open for a job that's a good fit. But in the meantime, at least I'll be able to pay my rent.

I hope you've gotten over being angry with me. I know you're not happy I'm here, but I hope that changes. When you asked me what I was doing here, I told you I came for you. That was only partly true. I also came

Me: for me. I missed you. I wanted to try to make things right with you. I wanted you to know where my feelings were. I've done so many dumb things in my life, but I really, REALLY hope this isn't one of them.

Anyway, good news about my job, huh? I don't know what your work schedule is like, but if you're around, would you like to celebrate my newfound employment? I can't really afford to go out to dinner, but I have the ingredients for a good stir-fry and you know you can use more veggies in your diet. Let me know if you're interested. See ya soon.

Chapter 14

Angus

After reading Charlotte's text, I threw my phone on my bed, left the bedroom, and shut the door harder than necessary. Then I felt a little foolish. I was behaving like a teenage valley girl, and there was no one here to appreciate the tantrum.

I slouched down on the couch and ran my hands through my hair, resisting the urge to pull it.

Not only had Charlotte come all the way to Kansas City much to my dismay, now she was living in my apartment complex. Why couldn't she have listened to me and gone home where she belonged. Was she trying to ruin me?

I let out a growl and then kinda hated myself. When had I become so melodramatic? I had spent so much time patiently waiting for Chuck to come around. I hadn't spent that time wringing my hands or pulling out my hair. I'd simply waited. Why, now that Chuck was here, did I feel like breaking dishes or punching a wall?

Maybe I should find another place to live.

Suddenly I wanted to know how close she actually was. I retrieved my phone off the bed and walked out the front door. I didn't even bother with shoes. I turned right, past my car in the parking lot, and followed the sidewalk. My building faced C, which meant D sat diagonally from mine. I craned my neck to see which second-floor apartment door had number 213 on the front.

There it was. And not far from where I stood was the CR-V with California plates. She was probably in that apartment right now, waiting to see how I'd respond to her invitation for stir-fry.

I shoved my hands in my pockets and looked up at the door. It would be so easy. I could walk up the steps and knock on her door. The fact that I'd come without a jacket or shoes would tell her I hadn't wasted a minute coming to her. I wouldn't have to say a word. I could just take her in my arms.

It was hard not to think about how it had felt to hold her. She was the tallest girl I'd ever kissed. I had wondered if it would be strange, but it wasn't. It was like we had been made for each other. It would feel good to erase the disappointment I'd seen on her face when I'd told her she should go home.

The cold sidewalk chilled my feet through their socks and a sharp, November wind pushed my shirt against my back.

It was so tempting. I could almost feel the pull from her front door. It would be so easy to give in to it. But easy didn't mean right and I had to do what was right for me, no matter how hard it was. The right thing was for me to protect myself from my feelings for Charles. What if I walked up there and opened myself up again and things didn't work out? She might not find a real job here and how long would she be satisfied cooking at a hotel restaurant before she was bored and wanted to go back to her good job and her family? Did Chuck even know her own feelings? Was I just the safety net that felt comfortable after years of losing so many times? How often are people happy about the consolation prize?

I dug in my pocket for my key when I got back to my apartment. The only thing I found was my cell phone and a few coins. I was locked out.

"See, Chuck, you're always causing me trouble," I said as I hurried to Daphne's office to see about a spare key.

Later that night, as I stared at the unmoving ceiling fan above my head, I realized I hadn't responded to Charlotte's text. I flipped on the lamp and re-read the text before I typed in a response.

Me: Charles, I'm happy you got a job if that's what you want, but I still think you should go back to Jayne Fife. You loved your job and you should get it back while you can. You're wasting your time here.

My thumb hovered over the send button. Why was she forcing me to be a jerk? I didn't want to hurt her. I deleted what I'd written and started over.

Me: Sorry I didn't get back to you sooner. I'm sure I'm too late for stir-fry. I had a crazy night tonight. Good luck at your new job.

I pushed the send button.

"Dr. Barclay, come on in." It still gave me a little thrill to hear myself called Dr. Barclay.

"Dr. Winters." He stood and shook my hand.

"I wanted you to take a look at this." Dr. Winters was the

physician overseeing my hip fellowship. I had shadowed him several times and had even watched him perform two hip replacements. The older man stood with his hands folded behind his back, looking over the glasses that rested low on his nose.

Dr. Winters was a small man, bald and wiry, with quick, sure movements. Despite his diminutive stature, he commanded respect and I felt my pulse quicken.

"What are we looking at?" I asked, standing beside him.

"Look at this hip socket and tell me what you see."

I wiped my suddenly clammy hands on my white coat and took a step forward, hoping I wouldn't fail this impromptu test. I studied the x-rays for a moment before I spoke.

"It looks like there are some abnormalities right in here." I made a circular motion around the hip joint.

"Can you elaborate?"

I studied the x-ray several more seconds. "It looks like there's deterioration in the femoral head and a buildup of fluid."

"That's right. The patient is a six-year-old male suffering from pain in the hip, thigh, and knee. They're coming in for an appointment with me this afternoon at two-thirty. I'd like you to take these to your office, do a little research, and meet me back here at two so we can go over your findings before they arrive."

I pulled the x-rays off the light box and slid them into the large envelope Dr. Winters handed me.

"Dr. Barclay?" he said when I'd reached the door.

"Yes?"

"This is going to be your case. I'll be a consulting doctor, but this boy now belongs to you."

"Thank you, doctor."

I felt a punch of adrenalin as I walked back to the office I shared with two other fellowship residents. My own case. A six-year-old boy who needed my help. I closed the door and began my research.

I felt confident as I knocked on Dr. Winters's door. I had spent the last couple of hours studying what could be wrong with my new patient, and I was eager to have Dr. Winters confirm my diagnosis.

"Come in, Dr. Barclay. Have a seat. Tell me what you've found."

"I believe the patient is suffering from Legg-Calve-Perthes disease."

"Hmm." Dr. Winters nod was slight, and it was hard to tell if he was agreeing, disagreeing, or encouraging me to continue. "Tell me more about this condition."

"Legg-Calve-Perthes disease is caused when there is insufficient blood-flow to the upper growth plate of the thigh. It causes the femoral head, or the ball of the hip joint, to deteriorate and it's painful. It often presents in children, especially males, so the patient is a good candidate for the disease. Of course, I'd like to examine the patient myself."

"Indeed. And you shall in about fifteen minutes." I wanted him to tell me I was right, but he just tapped his fingers together for a few seconds. "If you're correct, what would be your course of treatment?"

"If it had been caught earlier, I'd have recommended a leg brace and physical therapy. If it had gone on longer, and the bone had deteriorated further, I'd have recommended

106

surgery. If my diagnosis is correct"—I looked at Dr. Winters, but his expression was giving me nothing—"I think the patient is at a stage that will require traction before we put him in a brace, but not so severe as to need surgery."

"Why do you think that?"

I was starting to sweat. I stood and put the x-rays up on the light box and flipped the switch. Dr. Winters joined me in front of it. "There appears to be a buildup of fluid around the joint. I don't think anti-inflammatories would be enough to resolve it. By putting the patient in traction, we can calm the inflammation. We need to do that so the brace can contain the femoral head in the socket so it can begin healing."

Dr. Winters smiled. "Very impressive. I think you're ready to meet Braxton Chandler."

"Thank you, Dr. Winters." It was difficult not to grin. Not only did I have my own patient, but it appeared that Dr. Winters agreed with my diagnosis.

Braxton and his parents arrived at Dr. Winters' office a few minutes later. Braxton's limp was noticeable, his face strained but smiling. His father lifted him onto his knee. His mother reached over and held his hand.

Dr. Winters introduced us and turned to me. "Dr. Barclay is working on his hip fellowship, so he and I will be working together for you, Braxton. Dr. Barclay?"

I explained the diagnosis and our plan for treatment. Mr. and Mrs. Chandler's expressions softened with relief, and I realized they had been completely in the dark. It felt good to be able to help them.

We made arrangements for Braxton to be admitted to the hospital at the beginning of the following week. He would remain in traction for at least seven days, maybe more if the swelling was stubborn. The Chandlers shook my hand as they left.

When they were gone, Dr. Winters patted me on the back and inclined his head. "Good work, Dr. Barclay. Good work."

I should have been tired when I pulled into the Milton parking lot. It was almost eleven o'clock, and I'd been working since four in the morning. After my consultation with Dr. Winters, I had worked six hours in the emergency room. I should have been ready to crash, but I felt happy and energetic. Braxton Chandler was my patient. I would be making the decisions on his treatment.

I turned the opposite way of my parking space and moved slowly through the lot until I saw it. Charlotte's car. I glanced up at the window of 213. The light was on. I could share my good day with Charles. I knew it would make her happy if I knocked on the door and told her about Braxton.

It would make me happy, too.

Suddenly I missed Charlie with a fierceness I hadn't allowed myself to feel for a long time. I could do something about it, but if I knocked on her door, we'd be opening a door I wasn't ready to walk through. I wasn't about to set myself up again.

I circled the parking lot, pulled into my space, and walked into my cold, dark apartment. I reheated leftover frozen pizza and watched the local news.

Chapter 15

Charlotte

"Two chocolate cheesecakes and one lemon mousse with raspberries." Andy, one of the waiters, slapped the counter as he walked by, and I pulled out two dessert plates and one martini glass. I drizzled chocolate sauce across the two plates with an artistic flourish and carefully slid a piece of cheesecake onto each plate. Then I fanned out a sliced strawberry on top. I filled the glass with lemon mousse and put a small wedge of caramel lace at the edge, along with two plump, red raspberries.

Boyd came by and looked over the desserts before Andy picked them up. "Looks good."

Andy put them on his tray and left, winking at me over Boyd's shoulder. I pretended like I hadn't noticed and turned back to Boyd. Andy had been trying to flirt with me for the past week. If I were interested in dating anyone but Angus, I would have been flattered. As it was, I found his attention to be more like that of a cricket when you're trying to fall asleep.

"Listen, Charlotte, your desserts are lovely, but you need to practice on the parmesan curls. You're mangling them. Our diners have come to expect their Caesar salads to look a certain way, and parmesan crumbles simply do not pass as parmesan curls. Feel free to practice to your heart's content."

"What do you want me to do with the ones I mess up?"

"Don't mess up."

"Oh. I'll try not to." I felt my face turn red.

He waved me off with a loose wrist. "I'm kidding. I'm kidding. Don't take it so personally. You'll get it figured out."

I sort of smiled. "I'll keep working on it."

"Put the ones you mess up in a bag, and we'll use it in a sauce."

I pulled out a huge wedge of aged parmesan. My arm trembled as I slowly pulled the cheese slicer across the surface, leaving behind a trail of crumbled cheese. Would I ever get long curls of parmesan the way Boyd did? I'd been practicing on them for a week now with no noticeable improvement.

When I had arrived at Escape with two other temporary employees, Boyd had assigned me to "the pantry." I imagined a pantry like at home, and pictured myself spending two weeks stacking canned goods on shelves. "The pantry" turned out to be a wonderful assignment—except for parmesan curls—since its purpose was to make the salads and desserts. For a week now I'd been making garden and Caesar salads and plating cheesecakes and mousses and tortes. Another temp had been assigned to chop vegetables while the third had been assigned to wash dishes. I felt terrible for the dishwasher, as her shift lasted longer than ours and every time she walked through, her clothes were wet and she looked like she'd stepped out of a sauna. I had even asked Boyd if I should trade off with her every other day, but he said my desserts looked too good to mess with. I was secretly relieved, even though I wondered if she might make better parmesan curls.

"Let me show you a trick the girl before you used." Andy stepped around the counter and took the cheese slicer out of my hand. He leaned in close, his voice conspiratorial. I leaned back, putting a little distance between Andy's minty breath and my ear. "Don't let Boyd see this. He thinks everyone should be able to make curls with a cheese slicer, but Heather used a potato peeler and said it was much easier."

Andy pulled a potato peeler out of the pocket of his waiter's apron and held it up before pulling the cheese across the cutting board and slicing a perfect curl.

"Wow. Let me try that."

"I think it's the swiveling action of the blade. Look at you." He held up the parmesan curl I'd just cut and admired it before he plopped it in his mouth.

"Why would Boyd care how I make the curls?" I asked, slicing another pale yellow coil.

"It's Boyd. There's no explaining why he thinks the way he does."

"Thanks for sharing the tip."

"No problem. You sure I can't convince you to go with some of us to Big Red's after the restaurant closes?" This was the third night this week that Andy had invited me to join some of the staff at a bar around the corner.

"I'm sure. I've got to get home."

Andy peered at me closely. "Ah, I get it. You've got a man to get home to. I shoulda guessed."

Of course I didn't. At least not a man at home. But I did have a man in my apartment complex, which was why I wasn't interested in flirting or hanging out with another guy, so I decided to take the easy, slightly truth-bending way out.

"Yeah, I don't think he'd be thrilled if I joined you. But I do appreciate the offer."

Andy saluted me and headed out to the dining room. I thought about what I'd said as I sliced enough parmesan curls to get us through the rest of the night. Was it true? Would Angus be less than thrilled if I were to go out with another guy? Or would he be relieved?

It hurt to not know the answer.

"Another Saturday night in the books." Boyd flaccidly high-fived two of the waiters and one of the chefs as he walked through the kitchen. "Great night of service, people. Now finish cleaning up and get out of here."

I removed my chef coat and hung it on a hook around the corner from the pantry.

"You did well this week, Charlotte."

"Thank you."

"Did you get your meal tonight?" Each employee in the restaurant was compensated one meal per eight-hour shift.

"I had a bowl of lobster bisque and a roll."

"That's not a full meal, you know."

"I wasn't that hungry, and it was pretty busy."

"Jim?" Boyd clapped his hands together three times. "Please put together a molasses and walnut chicken for Charlotte to take with her."

"You want the fingerling potatoes and roasted vegetables with it?"

"You don't have to . . ."

Boyd interrupted me. "Yes, she wants everything. Be generous." He turned to me. "Take it home and share it with your honey."

I glanced around the kitchen, looking for Andy. "Now don't be upset with Andy for spilling the beans. Everyone around here was wondering whether you were single or not."

I didn't correct him. "Thanks."

Sweet and nutty aromas filled my car, and I realized I was starving. I was surprised to see Angus's car in the parking lot and even more surprised to see a light on in his apartment.

Maybe I was intoxicated by the delicious smells or perhaps I was fed up with the whole situation. I had been in Kansas City for three weeks and had seen Angus less than half a dozen times. I hadn't moved this far from home to spend all my time alone.

Indignation made me brave. I locked the car and carried the bag from Escape to Angus's front door and knocked.

It took Angus a minute to get to the door. He stood in front of me in jeans and an Avett Brothers concert t-shirt. His feet were bare.

"Hey, we went to that concert together." I inclined my head toward his shirt.

"Charlotte, do you know what time it is?"

"No." I quickly calculated what time it must be in my mind. The restaurant closed at ten. I cleaned the pantry, waited a few minutes for Jim to pack my meal, and drove home. Yikes.

"It's almost eleven."

"Sorry. It's just that they gave me a meal at the restaurant and it's way more than I can eat alone, so I thought I'd share. They even sent dessert."

"What restaurant?"

"Escape. Remember? I'm working there."

"Oh, right."

"Angus, I'm freezing and the food is probably getting cold. Can I please come in?"

He hesitated a moment and then stepped aside so I could walk past him.

"Are you hungry?"

"I already had dinner." He followed me to the kitchen counter.

"What time?"

"About six."

"That was almost five hours ago. You're probably hungry again, so this can be your midnight snack. Even though it's not quite midnight yet. Anyway, they sent way too much for me and I know you like good food and theirs is awesome, so I thought we could share."

I unpacked the food and opened the cartons so the delicious aroma filled the air. I knew I was babbling, but I wasn't sure how to stop. I pulled plates down from the cupboard and kept talking.

"I'm starving. I ate a bowl of soup at around four. You'd think working in a restaurant that you'd get immune to the smells, but so far I haven't. They were serving this seared scallop dish tonight that looked incredible, but they ran out of scallops around nine. Check out this cheesecake. I sliced the strawberries for it myself."

I glanced up at Angus and was surprised to see him smiling. Had I seen his smile since I arrived in town?

"What?"

He shook his head. "You can stop talking. I'm not going to kick you out."

"Really?"

"Now that my mouth is watering, there's no way I'm letting you go eat it alone."

I smiled. "Hopefully it tastes as good as it smells."

114

We divided up the food and carried our plates to the living room. A medical journal was open on the couch, so I sat in a chair across from him.

"Reading anything good?"

"Just studying up on treatments for a patient."

"Ooh. That sounds so doctorly. What kind of patient?"

For the next hour, we talked about our jobs. Angus told me about a six-year-old boy who had been assigned to him. He had an unusual condition in his hip that Angus had correctly diagnosed. I told him about the restaurant and how tonight had been the night I finally mastered parmesan curls.

I thought the story was amusing, but when I finished telling him about my work in the pantry, he looked serious.

"Chuck, you shouldn't be doing this."

I pushed around a piece of graham cracker crust with my fork. "Doing what?"

"Working at a restaurant."

"It's not so bad. I'm sure I'd feel differently if I were the one who'd been assigned to wash dishes, but the pantry's all right. Besides, I've got to pay the bills and I've got to eat. Kills two birds with one job. And where else could I work that lets me eat like this?"

The room was quiet and tense. We had spent a pleasant hour together, and I didn't want it spoiled with talk of me going back to San Francisco.

Angus sighed. "It's just . . ."

"Listen," I interrupted him, scooting to the edge of my chair and stacking my dessert plate onto my dinner plate. "I'm really tired. I'm going to head home."

Angus gathered his plates and followed me to the kitchen. "I'll take care of those."

I didn't argue with him. I wanted to leave before our

discussion turned into a debate. If I left now, I could think about the pleasant conversation and Angus smiling and even laughing.

"Thanks. I guess I'll see you around."

Angus shoved his feet into a pair of shoes by the front door. "What are you doing?" I asked.

"I'm walking you home."

"You don't have to do that. My apartment is just on the other side of that building."

"I know."

"I can make it alone."

"I'm sure you can. Let's go."

Angus shoved his hands in his pockets and we walked to my door. "Thanks for dinner, Charlie," Angus said as I unlocked my door.

"You're very welcome."

I went to the bedroom window and watched Angus walk back to his apartment. He glanced across the courtyard at my window and I took a step farther into the shadows. I felt a little jolt of excitement that he had figured out which apartment was mine.

Chapter 16

Charlotte

B oyd didn't mind if I saved my meal until the end of the
shift and then took it home with me. He always made
sure I took home a generous portion, including dessert. I
wanted to duplicate the comfortable evening Angus and I had
shared over molasses and walnut chicken, but for four nights
in a row, his car was gone and his windows were dark. I took
the food home with me and ate alone.

On the fifth night, Angus's car was there. Since it was a
weeknight, the restaurant closed at nine. Even though it was
earlier, I lacked the bravado that had spurred me on before. I
almost talked myself out of knocking on Angus's door. In fact,
I went home and changed my clothes before I rallied enough
courage to walk to his apartment.

I held up the bag like a peace offering when I saw him.
"Butter crusted sea bass and carrot cake?"

"You don't have to share with me, you know. You could
get two meals out of it if you just took it home with you."

I smiled. "I know. But that wouldn't be much fun."

"Come in."

"They served a chocolate and macadamia nut pie the other night that I thought you'd like, but you weren't home to share it, so of course I finished it myself. Sorry."

"It sounds good, but you're the one who loves the chocolate and nut pie, remember?"

"You like it too."

"Not like you do. I'd have felt guilty if I took any of that from you."

"It was good. Maybe they'll have it again before the job ends."

"Carrot cake sounds just as good to me. How much longer are you working there?"

"Only two more days. I'm going to miss this food."

Angus licked the serving spoon and put it in the sink. "Yeah, me too. This has been a nice perk."

"And it's saved me money on groceries."

"It could have saved you even more if you didn't bring it over here."

I ignored him. "I'm not looking forward to going back to my own cooking."

"At least you're a better cook than me."

"It depends on if we're talking real, edible food or video game food." I couldn't even count the number of times Angus had beat me at *Cooking Mama*.

"True."

"But even my best cooking isn't like this."

We were mostly quiet while we ate, but it wasn't uncomfortable. When the food was gone, I gathered our plates and took them to the kitchen. Angus opened his laptop.

"You probably haven't seen your email tonight, have you?"

"No."

"We got an email from McKayla."

"*We* got an email? What do you mean we?"

"She sent it to both of us. Come see."

I sat on the couch, leaving several inches between us. I didn't want to scare him and break this tenuous thread I hoped we were spinning. Angus leaned a little toward me, holding the laptop so we could both see the screen.

I wanted to concentrate on the email McKayla had sent—it was full of news and had several pictures of Simon—but it was hard to think about anything when Angus's arm was a hair's breadth away from my own.

He started reading aloud.

Hey guys. How's the Midwest? I've been watching the temperatures, and it's way colder there than it is here. No thank you. I'll just stay right here. And don't expect me to visit you until the spring thaw. You know how much I hate being cold.

Great news! Connor got the promotion. He'll now have two guys reporting to him. He'll have to travel once in a while, which I'm not thrilled about, but they said it would only be a few times per year. It's not a huge raise, but hey, a raise is a raise, right?

Simon is pretty cute. He smiles all the time and he's a little chubster, as you can see from the pics. We were joking the other night that if he keeps going like this, we're going to have to put him on a diet. Just kidding, but check out those cheeks. Have you ever seen more kissable cheeks?

I know it's ridiculous because McKayla was talking about a baby's cheeks, but hearing Angus read about kissing while he was sitting so close made my mind wander a little. Okay, a lot.

I wondered if Angus's mind wandered, but he seemed unfazed and kept reading.

You both need to do a better job of keeping us posted. Mom said you got a job with some creative place, Charlie, but I have no idea what that means. Details, sister. Details.

Angus gave me a quizzical look.

"The temp company is called Creative Resource Solutions," I explained. "I didn't tell them it was a temp agency."

Angus shook his head a little and continued.

Angus, give us an update on doctoring and hips and stuff. I know you guys have some news. Stop being so stingy.

Anyway, here are some pictures of Simon for your enjoyment. I know I'm a little biased, but can you believe how adorable he is? Next time I'll send you a video of him laughing. It's about the cutest thing in the world. We love you both. McKayla, Connor and Simon Says.

There were three pictures of Simon. He was a chubby, adorable baby. "He's so cute."

There must have been a wistful note in my voice because Angus sat up straight, closed the laptop, and looked at me. "You should be with your family."

"Let's not do this, okay?"

"They don't even know where you're working. If you're having to mislead your family, it should be a clue that you're doing the wrong thing."

I shook my head. "I don't want them to worry."

"And what about Simon and Emily? You should be there.

You're missing out on important things."

"I said I don't want to do this."

"What are you going to do after next week? When this job ends?"

"They can send me out on something else."

"Charles, stop being so stubborn."

"I'm not the only one being stubborn." I folded my arms, but when I realized I was looking like a pouting child, I unfolded them and stood to leave. "Look, we're both tired. I'm going to bed."

Angus followed me to the door. "Sorry. I didn't mean to jump on you. I just want you to be happy." He followed me out his front door and I could tell he planned to walk me home again. I appreciated the gesture, but I wanted this topic of conversation to end.

Angus had other ideas. "Look, Charlotte, I don't want to be the reason you miss out on so much."

The air was cold and I shivered. "I decided to come here. You didn't ask me to, so you can stop feeling guilty about it."

"What if you don't find a job you like?"

I shrugged. "Then I'll do something I don't like."

Angus stopped walking. "Charlotte, I'm not kidding." He didn't have to tell me. I could tell by his tone he was serious.

I kept walking. "Neither am I."

Boyd asked me to stay for two more days, which I happily agreed to. It meant two more good meals, crème brulee, and chocolate hazelnut cake. Angus wasn't home to share them with me, and after our last conversation, I wasn't sure he would have let me in anyway.

Mark at Creative Resource Solutions sent me to a construction equipment company where I answered phones for two days. It was boring work that left me more tired than eight hours at Escape. I was glad it was only a two day job.

I had no work for three days after that. I called on a few job prospects, bought a few inexpensive groceries, and tried to read a book. I had read the same page four times when Hallmark called.

Chapter 17

Angus

"Knock knock." I walked into Braxton's hospital room. I could tell the mood was tense before anyone answered.

"Hi, Dr. Barclay." Mrs. Chandler stood and shook my hand. Braxton lifted his hand off the blanket in a lukewarm wave.

"How ya doing there, champ?" I ruffled his pale hair, but his large, gray eyes never left the television. I checked the position and weight on the traction apparatus then perched myself on the edge of the bed. Braxton still didn't look at me.

I glanced at the television on the wall behind me. "*The Flintstones*? I didn't even know they were on anymore. This is probably my favorite cartoon of all time."

"It's okay." Braxton's mood was sullen.

"Have you seen the one where Fred becomes a movie star?"

"No."

"That one's my favorite. Let me know if it comes on. Maybe I can come watch it with you." His eyes didn't leave the television.

"You getting used to this thing?"

Braxton shrugged. He had been in traction for four days, and the progression of his emotions had gone from fear to curiosity to boredom. Today he seemed despondent.

"I know it's not much fun to stay in bed like this, but even though it seems like you're not doing anything but watching television, some really cool things are happening inside your body. Want me to tell you about them?"

Braxton shrugged again, but said, "Sure."

"Your hip has been sore for a long time, hasn't it?"

He nodded.

"That's because of this big bone here." I touched his thigh. "It's called the femur. The top of it is shaped like a ball, and it fits in the hip socket like this." I made a fist with my left hand and put it in the curved palm of my right hand. Braxton tore his gaze away from Fred and Wilma to look. "The part that looks like a ball got sick, so it quit working right. Then everything around it felt sorry for it, so they jumped in to help."

"How did they help?"

"All those little tissues inside thought they could make it feel better by swelling up and filling up the space around your hip. Kinda like a bunch of pillows trying to make it a more comfortable place. They were trying to give your bone a chance to get better."

"Why didn't it work?"

"Well, they thought they were doing a good thing, but actually, it made it harder for your bone to fit in the right place. It has to fit in there or it can't get better, so we're helping it. This is pulling on your leg just enough so all the stuff that swelled up and tried to help can calm down and get some rest and go back to the right size. When that happens, your bone will be able to fit back in the place where it's supposed to be."

"When can we take it off?"

"We're not sure yet. Usually it takes about a week for the swelling to go down. Sometimes, if the tissues are trying to be extra helpful and don't want to give up, it takes a little longer."

"How much longer?" Now it was Mrs. Chandler asking, and I detected a note of desperation in her voice.

"I think two weeks would be the absolute longest." She blew out a little breath. "But that's unusual. I'd guess a week to ten days would be more like it."

Braxton let out a long raspberry sigh. "Ten whole days? I'm gonna go crazy."

Mrs. Chandler and I laughed, and the heavy mood in the room lightened a little.

She squeezed Braxton's hand. "He's not the only one."

"I know it's rough to be in here, but remember what's happening in there. We want to get you all better so you can run and play and do all the things you haven't been able to."

"Will it hurt to walk after that?" Braxton asked.

"Probably a little. But tomorrow someone's going to come in and measure you for a brace. It's this cool thing that will hold your hip in the right place so it won't hurt and so your bone can get completely better."

Braxton nodded and turned back to *The Flintstones*.

I patted his leg and started for the door. Mrs. Chandler followed me into the hall.

"Thanks for explaining that to him."

"Of course. It's hard for a six-year-old to be tied down like this. I'd have gone crazy myself."

"You missed his fit this morning. He was in a horrible mood and threw his breakfast onto the floor. I guess I need to find him something to occupy his time. Hopefully it's only for a week."

I gave her a sympathetic smile and hoped right along with her.

I've always considered myself a nice guy. Maybe that's why my interactions with Charlotte were bothering me. I didn't like the way things had gone and even though I thought Charles should be in San Francisco, I had to admit, it was pretty nice having her close. But I couldn't make this about what was convenient and pleasant for me. I needed to think about her. How long would it be before she resented me for being the reason she left her great job? How long before she wondered if it had been worth it to leave her family, especially her niece and nephew, to sit around lonely while I worked long hours? I was surprised she'd lasted this long.

But Charles was stubborn and five weeks later, she was still here. I could have continued to wait her out, but Thanksgiving was two days away, and I had no idea what Charlotte would be doing. Sometimes her car was in the lot and sometimes it wasn't, so I was pretty sure she hadn't gone home for the holiday. How could I let her spend it alone?

Neither of us had ever been away from home on Thanksgiving. This would be a first for both of us. Logic would say we should spend it together. After all, we're friends, right? But still I hesitated. I didn't want to give her another reason to stay away from her real home.

But I didn't want an enemy either. Sitting beside

Charlotte while we read McKayla's email had been a light bulb moment for me. I didn't want to lose my friendship with the Emersons, Charlotte included. They were like family to me. But they were an actual family to each other, and if I didn't salvage my friendship with Charlotte, I'd probably lose them all.

My last conversation with Charlotte kept running through my mind, and every time it did, I felt like a bigger jerk. Chuck had generously shared food from her job and she'd been pleasant and cheerful. She hadn't been pushy at all. In fact, it had started to feel almost like the old days. Maybe that was the problem. How was I supposed to get her to move back home if we grew too comfortable here?

But this was Thanksgiving, and the thought of her spending it alone ate at me. I knew I would hate myself if I let that happen. Maybe I could set aside my worries and give in just this once.

. Me: Are you going home for Thanksgiving?

Charlotte: No.

Me: Your family must be bummed.

Charlotte: Probably.

Me: Have you checked on flights? There still might be time.

Charlotte: I'm not going.

I've never been great at reading people's moods through texts, but Charlotte sounded a little snippy. Part of that was probably my fault. Maybe all of it. Further evidence that I had probably hurt her. I felt terrible.

Me: I'm not going home either. Mom was disappointed.

Charlotte: That's too bad.

127

Me: I'm scheduled to work a half day.

I waited for a reply and when twenty minutes had passed with no response, I tried again.

Me: I work until one.

She still didn't text back. I considered leaving it there. I could sooth my conscience by telling myself I had tried to arrange something with her for Thanksgiving, but that wouldn't make me feel better if she ended up spending the day alone.

I felt like smacking myself in the head. I was lying to myself. Of course I was worried about her being lonely and far away from home, but I actually longed to spend the day with her. I didn't want to be alone either and we were friends. Why not spend it together?

Maybe it would even give me a chance to let her know why I wanted her to go home. If she understood I was thinking of her best interests, maybe she wouldn't be so stubborn.

Me: If you don't have plans, we could have Thanksgiving together. As friends. No sense two friends spending the day a hundred yards apart and alone, right?

I suspect my overuse of the word friends should have been a clue to me that Charlotte wasn't the only one who needed reassurance that this was a friendly invitation. There was still no response and the entire time I casted a woman's wrist, I kicked myself for extending the invitation. When I had a moment, I texted her again.

Me: No worries if you already have plans. It was just an idea.

It was late afternoon when Charlotte finally replied.

Charlotte: Sorry. I was at work and I couldn't check my phone. Thanksgiving sounds great. Do you have time to go grocery shopping together or should I take care of it?

Me: I could go if we went during lunch tomorrow.

Charlotte: I'll be at work then. I'll just go tomorrow night and we can cook it together after you get off on Thursday. If you don't mind eating dinner in the evening instead of the afternoon.

Me: I don't mind. Where are you working?

Charlotte: Hallmark, but it's not what you think. It's just a temporary thing at Crown Center. I'll tell you about it on Thursday. Let's eat at my place so I can have some of the food going before you get there.

Me: Sounds good. But don't do it all. Let me help.

Charlotte: Any special food requests?

Me: I trust you.

Me again: Just so we're clear, this is because we're friends. It doesn't mean I think you should stay here. I still think you should move back home.

There was a long pause, and I wished I could take the last text back.

Charlotte: You've made your position very clear.

Chapter 18

Charlotte

"I've got a rack of pretty papers and a box of buttons," I said to the seven children seated around my table. "Each of you need to pick out 15 origami papers and 10 of these tiny buttons.

"What about the star?" asked a pretty girl with cornrows.

"When your tree is finished, I've got a special bag of stars and you can choose one."

The children scrambled to the rack of papers, eager to be first to choose, even though it didn't matter. There were plenty of papers to go around.

This wasn't exactly the kind of job I'd been hoping for when I applied at Hallmark, but it was a foot in the door, and I needed the money. On top of that, my first couple of days had been fun.

Imaginarium was a child's dream. Instead of being dragged all over the giant shopping plaza while their parents shopped, children were brought to Imaginarium, where they could make craft projects and watch movies. The walls were black and filled with glow-in-the-dark chalk drawings. Colorful pendant lights illuminated each station. A large corner was filled with bright beanbags and a television the size of a small movie screen. I had been hired to work one of the craft tables through the holiday rush. Today we were making a rolled paper Christmas tree.

"Excuse me." A Chinese boy tapped my arm. "Why are we making a Christmas tree? Shouldn't we be making something for Thanksgiving?"

"Well, Thanksgiving is tomorrow, so if we made a Thanksgiving project, you'd only have one day to enjoy it. But since we're doing a Christmas tree, you'll be able to hang it up the day after Thanksgiving and enjoy it for a whole month."

"Ah." He pointed his finger at me. "That makes very good sense." He carried his papers to the table and waited for the rest of the children to make their selections.

For the next hour, we rolled papers and glued them to a foam core back. Then the children decorated their trees with the buttons and finally picked out a star from the bag of jeweled stars.

I worked with five sets of children throughout the day, and when I left, I was tired but happy. The children were an entertaining and challenging mix of well-behaved, quizzical, precocious, and downright difficult. It was harder than the pantry at Escape, but much more enjoyable than the construction equipment company. I refused to compare it to Jayne Fife.

I stopped at the grocery store on the way home. That was almost worse than an eight hour shift since it seemed that all of Kansas City had decided to do their Thanksgiving grocery shopping at the same time. And possibly at the same grocery store. It was so crowded, and for people who were supposed to be feeling thankful, most of them were pretty grouchy.

I collapsed onto the couch after I unloaded the groceries and opened my laptop. Since I wouldn't be with my family tomorrow, I wanted to send them a message. I began typing an email.

Dear Family,

Today will be the first Thanksgiving we haven't been together, and I'm sitting here tonight wondering if I should have accepted Will and Gina's offer to fly me home. Thank you both for the offer. I definitely would have taken you up on it if I weren't coming home in just four weeks for Christmas.

I will be here thinking about you tomorrow. Angus is coming over after he finishes at the hospital, and we're cooking Thanksgiving dinner together, so at least it will feel like I'm with some family.

I imagine you'll probably read this during the Thanksgiving circle, so I want to tell you a few of the things I'm thankful for this year. Forgive me if my list is long, but since I'm not there, I'm giving myself permission to go on longer than if I were there.

I'm thankful that you all were willing to support me going to Scotland, even though you were worried. That trip was good for my soul and if I ever win the lottery, I'm taking you all to the Isle of Lewis.

I'm thankful for the cutest niece and nephew in the world. Man, I cannot wait until I get to hold and play with you two cute little people.

I'm thankful for Flynn. He turned out to be such a wise, unselfish friend.

I'm thankful for Will and Gina and McKayla and Connor. I'm so lucky to have such wonderful brothers and sisters.

I'm so thankful for Mom and Dad. Sorry I've been such a worry to you this year. I'll try to make next year worry-free.

I'm thankful to be here so Angus doesn't have to spend Thanksgiving alone.

Tears were streaming down my face, and I wiped them onto my sleeve. In spite of slashed tires, a distant Angus, job insecurities and homesickness, I'd mostly kept it together since I arrived in Kansas City. I was due for a good cry, and it would be better to have it tonight than tomorrow when Angus was here. If I cried in front of him, it would convince him he was right about me going home.

No, I would cry tonight, and then tomorrow I would be on top of my game. I finished my email home.

I love you all and hope you have the best day ever. Enjoy the day and eat an extra scoop of Mom's stuffing for me.

Love, Charlotte

Angus arrived just before two, freshly showered and looking way too handsome in khakis, a green plaid button-down shirt and a navy pullover sweater. His hair was damp, and he smelled clean and spicy. If he hadn't made such a point of letting me know we were eating together as friends, I might have thought he was trying to smell good for me. Oh well. I'd enjoy it either way.

With only two of us, the portions we made were small, but we still had to make everything. Angus took a small turkey to cook at his apartment and we baked a pumpkin and apple pie in my oven.

"Tell me about your job with Hallmark," Angus said

as he cut up potatoes.

I whisked Mom's cream sauce recipe as it slowly heated on the stove. "Have you heard of Imaginarium? At Crown Center?" He hadn't, so I told him about the job and the crafts the children did. "It's kind of a glorified babysitting job while their parents do their Christmas shopping, but most of the kids are cute and it's fun."

"And you're using your artistic talents."

"Sort of. It's more crafty than artistic."

"There's a difference?"

"I hope so. Anyone can roll up paper and glue buttons. I hope not everyone can do what I do, or I'm pretty dispensable." I pulled out my phone and showed Angus a few of the trees the children had made.

"Is this a permanent job?"

I searched Angus's face to see if this was a loaded question, but I couldn't read anything there other than curiosity.

"I'm working until the twenty-third. I'll fly home on Christmas Eve. I don't know if they'll want me to come back after Christmas or not."

"Do you hope they do?"

I thought about it. "It's certainly better than some things I could be doing, but I'd rather be designing cards or gifts for Hallmark. But at least my foot is in the door. My check is signed by Hallmark. That counts for something, right?"

"Today crafts with kids. Tomorrow get well cards. I'm glad you're going home for Christmas."

Everything we said was so fraught with uncertainty. I wanted to analyze every sentence and know what meaning Angus was attaching to it, but I didn't want to ask, so I just kept the conversation moving. "What are you doing for Christmas?"

134

"I have to work, so Mom and Dad are coming out here."

"Oh, good. I was worried you'd be here alone." It had almost kept me from booking my ticket.

I turned off the stove and poured the cream sauce over a pan of green beans. "I have to work on Christmas evening, but I'll have the morning with them and they're staying for a little over a week, so we'll get to spend some time together."

"Are they staying with you?"

"I'm thinking I might sleep on the couch and give them my bed. Save them the cost of a hotel."

"I'll be gone. They should stay here. Then they won't have to pay for a hotel and you won't have to sleep on a couch and be exhausted for work."

Angus thought for a moment. "How long are you going to be gone?"

"I'm staying for three weeks. Mia and Graham are getting married December 27 and Kyle and . . . Oh, did you get invited to Kyle and Wyatt's wedding?"

"Yeah. Thank goodness I'll be here working. Please tell me you're not going?"

I shrugged. "They invited me. And it will probably be really nice."

An awkward silence followed. I knew Angus didn't approve of me going to exes' weddings. He had seen me struggle through them more than once. But this was different, wasn't it? This time I could go knowing I was in love with someone else. But I wasn't sure how that someone else felt about me anymore, so maybe it wasn't so different.

"I'm sorry I won't be there." His voice was quiet and serious.

"Yeah, too bad. Of course they'll have fantastic food. They'll be serving a lot of important people."

Angus huffed and put down his knife. "Charles, that's not why I wish I could be there."

"It's not?"

"No. I wish I could be there so I could talk you out of going. It'll be hard for you."

I shook my head. "I'm over him, Angus. And I like Wyatt. I'll be okay."

"Don't go. Send them a card. Let them get on with their lives without you having to act happy for them."

"But I am happy for them."

"I wish you wouldn't go, but suit yourself."

Angus was so frustrating. How had he managed to turn an offer of a bed for his parents into a guilt-trip about attending Kyle and Wyatt's wedding? "We weren't talking about the wedding. I was offering my apartment to your parents."

Angus's smile was sheepish. "Sorry. Yeah. They'd probably prefer that to a hotel, and Mom already said they refused to kick me out of my bed. This would keep us from fighting about it."

"I'll change the sheets and leave you my key before I go."

Angus cleared his throat, a habit I recognized. Angus often cleared his throat when he wanted to say something and he wasn't sure how it would be received. "Have you considered staying when you go home?"

I ignored him while I pulled the pies out of the oven and placed them on a towel on the counter. When they were out of my hands and I was sure I wouldn't be tempted to throw one of them at Angus, I responded. "I have a great idea." Angus looked curious. "Why don't you remember that I'm a grown up and let me decide where I'm going to live." I tried to keep my voice light, but he must have known he'd touched a nerve because he held up his hands in surrender.

"Okay, okay. I get it. No more pushing you to go home."

"Thank you."

"At least for today."

I shook my head. "Why don't you take your bossy, stick-your-nose-in-Charlotte's-business self in and turn on the football game."

Angus found the game, and we worked and watched together for a while without talking. It was actually nice to be together without listening to him lecture me about going home.

We turned off the television and ate dinner at about six. Angus said a prayer over our modest feast and offered thanks for the food, for our families, and for good friends.

With only two of us, dinner was over and my kitchen sparkling by eight o'clock.

"We should go to a movie," Angus said, taking me completely by surprise.

"That sounds fun."

An hour later we were sitting in a terrible movie about a man who'd crossed the mafia and had a hit out on him. It was supposed to be intense and exciting, but some of the lines were so poorly written it was difficult not to laugh. It didn't help that Angus would nudge me with every bad line. At one point the hero was eating an ice cream cone when the villain stepped up behind him. "You think this is a good time to be eating ice cream?" he asked in a menacing voice.

"As a matter of fact, I do." The hero had a defiant look on his face.

"Eat slowly, because every lick tastes like death."

Angus elbowed me at the same time that I snorted and collapsed into a fit of giggles.

"Shut her up," someone stage whispered behind us.

Angus waved his hand and whispered, "Sorry." Then he leaned over to me and through his laughter said, "Get control of yourself before you get me in a fight."

It was a struggle, but we managed to get through the rest of the movie without making a scene.

It was almost like the day had made Angus forget that he didn't want me here because as we walked to the car after the movie, he put his arm around me for a brief moment and squeezed my shoulder. "This was a nice day," he said, and then instantly dropped his arm and put his hands in his jacket pockets.

I wanted to link my arm through his and snuggle up to him, but I had learned the last night I saw him in San Francisco that it was a bad idea for me to push things. I didn't want to drive him away, so I put my hands in my pockets, smiled, and said, "It was a very nice day."

Chapter 19

Angus

I put Braxton Chandler's latest x-ray up on the light box for Dr. Winters to see. "It's going slower than I had hoped," I said. He studied the darker area around the hip socket and nodded.

"There has been some improvement in the inflammation, but I concur. Not enough to move him to a brace."

"I wanted to get your opinion before I go break the bad news."

"Bad news?"

"Braxton is having a hard time with the traction. He's so bored, he's acting out and it's been tough for him and his parents. Especially his mom."

Dr. Winters nodded. "It's hard to be tied down for that long. You should talk to the mother. See if you can find something that will help make these last several days a little more bearable." He looked again at the x-ray. "I think you're probably looking at four or five more days."

How was I going to break the news to Braxton and his mother? When I'd stopped by his room last night, she had followed me into the hall and joked about anesthetizing him for the remainder of the traction. He was sick of cartoons and movies and books.

It was only the day after Thanksgiving, but someone had decorated the nurses' station with red and silver tinsel. I glanced in a hospital room and saw that a patient had a small Christmas tree set up in the window.

And then I had an idea.

Although it seemed like a good idea, my first inclination was to ignore it. It would require Charlotte's help, and I was determined not to initiate too much contact with her. How could I get her to go back to San Francisco if she thought I needed her here? No. I could figure out something else without having to bother Charles.

I heard him before I reached the room. The sound was surprising because thus far, Braxton had demonstrated his unhappiness with his situation by being sullen or hostile. I stood outside the room and listened as he cried. His mother made soothing sounds, but nothing could console him. It was easier to ignore the anger and moodiness, but the broken-hearted weeping of a six-year-old was harder to take.

I took a deep breath and walked into the room. It was worse than I had thought. Braxton wasn't the only one crying. Tears were also streaming down his mother's cheeks. And now I was supposed to tell them they had four or five more days of this? I fixed an understanding smile on my face.

"Good morning, you two."

Mrs. Chandler quickly wiped away her tears. "Hi, Dr. Barclay."

"It looks like we're having a hard time in here."

"It was hard spending Thanksgiving in the hospital. Braxton missed playing with his cousins."

"I'm sorry about that, Braxton. Maybe you can have some of them come visit you."

Mrs. Chandler shook her head. "They're in Oklahoma. That's where we would have gone if we hadn't been here."

"Ah, that's rough. I'm sorry you missed that." I touched his arm. I could tell this sadness was different because he didn't pull away. "Hey, little man, would you mind if I borrowed your mom for a minute?"

He shook his head. Mrs. Chandler kissed his forehead and followed me into the hall.

"You don't have good news for me, do you?" she asked.

I didn't beat around the bush. "There's definite improvement, but he's going to need four or five more days."

She looked like she might cry again, but she nodded.

It was time to think about someone other than myself and what was easiest for me. "Mrs. Chandler, do you think he'd enjoy something artistic to do? Actually, I guess it's more crafty," I said, remembering Charlotte's explanation.

"He might."

"What if we made it a plea for his help? You know, give him something to think about and work toward?"

"What do you mean?"

I explained what I had in mind. Mrs. Chandler smiled and agreed.

"I think it would be better coming from you," she said.

"Let me call my friend and I'll stop back by later today."

Me: Charlotte, could you give me a call when you have a minute?

She called while I was in the cafeteria eating lunch.

"Thanks for calling me."

"Sorry it wasn't sooner. I had to wait for my group session to end."

I felt a twinge of hypocrisy that I was asking Chuck to help me out when most of what I had done since she arrived was try to get her to go home.

"I need to ask a favor."

"Sure. What do you need?" I felt grateful for Charlotte's willingness and glad she hadn't made me feel guilty for enlisting her help.

"Do you remember Braxton, the boy I told you is in traction?"

"The six-year-old, right?"

"He's having a hard time, and we decided today that he has to be in traction for four or five more days. I was wondering if you'd be willing to come and teach him how to make those rolled paper Christmas trees. I want to give him a job to make one for every patient's room on his floor. He needs to stay busy, and I want him to feel like he's doing something important to help other people have a good Christmas. I think that might help him get through the next few days."

"That's a great idea. I'd be happy to."

"I'll pay for the supplies. Just get what you need and let me know how much it is."

"Can he have a visitor this evening? I could come by when I get off," Charlotte said. "There's a craft store here at the Plaza that I can stop at after work. How many trees do you want him to make?"

"Let's get supplies for about fifteen and if he ta kes to it, we'll get more."

"This will be fun." Charles sounded genuinely excited and I felt a surge of gratitude for her kindness.

"Thanks, Chuck."

"I can't wait to meet him. I can be there by about seven. Will you be there or should I just go to his room?"

"I'm not sure if I'll be off yet or not. It depends on the emergency room. I'll let him know you're coming, and I'll try to meet you there, but if I can't, his room is 337."

I stopped by Braxton's room in the afternoon and let him know I had a friend coming by in the evening to see him.

"She's been my friend since a long time before you were even born, so please be extra nice to her, okay?"

"Is she your girlfriend?" Braxton smiled, something I hadn't seen for a few days.

"No. She's just my friend."

"She's a girl and she's your friend, so she's your girlfriend."

I laughed and his smile widened. His mom grinned at me across the bed.

"Just be nice to her and tomorrow you have to tell me the names of all *your* 'girlfriends'."

"I don't have any. I don't like girls."

"Well, I'll bet you'll like Charles."

"Charles? Your girlfriend's name is Charles?"

"Her name is Charlotte, but I call her Charles sometimes. And Charlie and Chuck. Come to think of it, I think you should call her Chuckers when she comes. She'll like that."

"I'm sure she will," said Mrs. Chandler.

"Chuck. Chuckers." Braxton tried out the names.

My Emergency Room shift was supposed to go from two to eight, but it was so quiet all afternoon that I thought I might be able to sneak out at seven to meet Charlotte. Unfortunately, seven seemed to be the appointed hour for a boy to break his wrist in a basketball game, a woman to cut her head on the corner of a cabinet, and a man to try to pass a marble-sized kidney stone. I couldn't even leave at eight because of a concussion and a sewing machine needle going through a thumb.

It was eight-forty when I finally headed to the third floor.

"Could you hold that, Dr. Barclay?"

I put my arm out to keep the elevator doors from closing on Mr. and Mrs. Chandler. When they were in the elevator, I pushed the button for the third floor.

"Your friend is an angel. She insisted we go out to dinner."

"Is she still up there with Braxton?"

"Yes."

"Good. I was afraid I'd missed her."

"It was nice for Shelly to get a little break," Mr. Chandler said, and Mrs. Chandler nodded.

As we neared Braxton's room, we heard him laugh. His parents stopped in the hall and exchanged a look of relief. I paused with them.

"Dr. Barclay picked the right person for this job," Charlotte said. "You're a pro."

"Do you think I'll have time to make one for every room?"

"I hope so. I feel sorry for any rooms that don't get a

144

Braxton original Christmas tree. Man, I love this one. Great color choices. If you have time after you make one for each of the hospital rooms, do you think you could make one for me? I'd like to have one of my own for when you're famous."

"Sure. Do you want to pick your favorite colors?"

"No way. I want you to pick them. You have such good taste."

"Thanks, Charlotte."

I stepped into the room. "Did I just hear you call her Charlotte? I thought we agreed you'd call her Chuck. Or Chuckers."

"She's too nice to call her those names."

"And too pretty," Mrs. Chandler said. Charles smiled at me from the other side of Braxton's bed, and I realized Mrs. Chandler was probably right. Charlotte was much too pretty to be called Chuckers. But Chuck would be a hard habit to break.

"Do you want to show Dr. Barclay what you're doing?" Charlotte asked Braxton.

Braxton pointed to a box of supplies on the floor and described the patterned origami paper and the colorful buttons. "Charlotte is bringing some stars tomorrow that look like jewels. She showed me a picture on her phone."

"Look how beautiful these two are," Charlotte said, and Braxton beamed.

"Those look great," Mr. Chandler said.

"He picked out those colors himself. He's got a good eye." Charlotte patted his leg.

"Charlotte said you want me to make one for every room on this floor."

"If you have enough time before you leave," I said. "It will be nice for every room to have a pretty Christmas decoration.

It might help some of the patients not be so sad they have to be in the hospital during the holidays."

"I'll have time." Braxton continued rolling a paper around a pencil while he talked. "Charlotte says I'll get faster when I make more. And she said she'll come help me again after she gets off work tomorrow."

"If that's okay with all of you." Charlotte looked around at our enthusiastic nods.

"We should probably let Charlotte go home now," Mr. Chandler said. "She's probably pretty tired."

"She's not tired," Braxton said. "She's just hungry. Her stomach has been growling like crazy."

"Maybe you should take her out to dinner," Mrs. Chandler said to Angus.

"Yeah," Braxton said. "Go get her some chicken nuggets."

We laughed.

"Do you think you can remember how to do this and show your mom?"

"Sure. But you'll still come back tomorrow, right?"

"Of course. I'll have to stop in to see your masterpieces."

Charlotte and I left together. I planned to follow Mrs. Chandler's advice and take Charles to get something to eat, but I didn't have a chance.

"Just in case you're wondering how to get out of taking me out for chicken nuggets, you can rest easy. I'm exhausted and there's plenty of turkey and rolls left. I'm just going to eat some leftovers and go to bed.

Since we had split the leftovers the night before, there wasn't even a reason to eat leftovers together.

Her dismissal left me feeling unmoored.

146

Chapter 20

Charlotte

"*C* ome in, Charlotte." Warren Osnes met me at the door of his office and shook my hand. "Have a seat. Thanks for making time to come see me before you leave town."

Mr. Osnes was a Staypuff Marshmallow of a man who worked in Human Resources at Hallmark. His office was in the Hallmark Building, walking distance from Imaginarium. His secretary had called yesterday to set up an appointment. Was it possible something had opened up in the design studio? Today had been my last day at Imaginarium. Tomorrow I would be flying home to spend Christmas with my family.

I superstitiously crossed my fingers. It would be wonderful to have a job with Hallmark to come back to instead of nothing but Creative Resource Solutions temporary positions.

"Cassie tells me you've done an outstanding job at Imaginarium."

"Thank you."

"It takes a special kind of person to work with so many children."

"I've enjoyed it."

"I'm glad to hear that. I've been looking over your application. It looks like you originally applied to work in our design department."

"That's where most of my experience is. In San Francisco, I was designing souvenirs."

"Interesting. It looks like you're certainly qualified. The only problem is . . ."

My heart fell. I didn't want to hear about problems. I wanted good news. I didn't want to have to sugarcoat my situation to everyone at home.

". . . we don't have any openings in the design department at the moment."

I tried to cover my disappointment with a smile, but it felt fake.

"I think that's why Bambie hired you for the temporary spot at Imaginarium. I think she wanted to keep you busy until a position opened up."

"It was definitely good to have a job through the holidays."

"Yes. Well, if you're interested, we'd like to have you come back to Imaginarium when you return in January. We're losing Crystal who is headed for Oklahoma State. Or is it The University of Oklahoma? I'm not sure. Oh well. It's one of those Oklahoma schools, and I'm pretty sure it isn't Oral Roberts. Anyway, she's leaving, and we need to fill her position. Cassie recommended we offer the position to you."

"Would I still be considered for a design job when

one comes available?"

"Oh, yes." His laugh filled his office. "That's part of our cunning plan."

I laughed with him.

"My first love is design, so I'm crossing my fingers"—I showed him my crossed fingers—"for something there, but I've enjoyed Imaginarium. Thank you for the offer."

We discussed when I'd return from California, and he shook my hand as I left.

It wasn't what I had hoped for, but I left smiling anyway. At least I was coming back to a job.

The sidewalk between my apartment and Angus's was treacherous. A three-day snowstorm had ended yesterday. Maintenance had shoveled the walks from doorways to the parking lot, but no one had shoveled the sidewalks through the courtyard. Snowshoes would have been ideal, but I didn't even own any snow boots. Hopefully my short Christmas list would remedy that.

"Oh, my goodness," Janice said when she opened the door. "Get in here and give me a hug."

Janice pulled me into Angus's apartment and hugged me tightly, swaying back and forth.

"How was your trip?"

"Easy peasy. They kept announcing delayed and canceled flights, and I thought for sure we'd be stuck somewhere because of the storm, but we had no problem at all. In fact, we landed fifteen minutes before we were scheduled to." I followed her to the living room. "Dave, look who's here."

"Charlie-girl. Good to see you." He hugged me, then held me at arm's length and winked at me. "You're a girl of surprises, aren't you?" I wondered what Angus had told them. Were they glad I was here or did they find it strange?

"I like to keep you on your toes, Dave."

"Come sit down," Janice said. She and Dave sat on the couch and I took the chair opposite them.

"I'm glad you got here before I leave tomorrow. I was hoping I'd be able to see you."

"We were too. And thank you for letting us stay in your apartment."

"Really, I don't mind if you come over tonight. I can sleep on the couch for one night."

"Not a chance," Dave said. "We're kicking Angus out to the couch for one night."

"You look good," I said to Dave. "How are you feeling?"

"I'm feeling good. Saw the doctor earlier this month and for now I'm cancer free."

"That's great news. I hope it stays that way. Have you seen Angus yet?"

"No. He had to work, so we took a cab from the airport," Janice said. "Angus hid the key for us."

"You should have said something. I could have come and picked you up."

"I'm sure you had plenty to do to get ready for your trip. I'll bet you're excited to see your family."

We caught up for a while. It made me even more excited to get home and see my family. It also reminded me how much I love Dave and Janice. At the moment, I loved them more than I loved Angus.

We had talked for over an hour and I knew Angus would be getting home soon. I didn't want to intrude on their reunion, so I stood to leave.

"I'm so glad I got to see you. I hope you have a great time."

"Where do you think you're going?" Dave said. "We're all going to dinner."

"We are?"

"That boy." Janice shook her head. "He was supposed to let you know we wanted to take you out to dinner tonight. We asked him to make a reservation at that restaurant where you worked."

I felt the color rise in my cheeks. Janice thought Angus had forgotten to tell me. I knew that was a possibility, but I also knew maybe he didn't want me to join them.

"Maybe we should call and check on the reservation," Dave said.

I pulled up the number on my phone and recited it to Janice so she could call. If he had made reservations for three, there was no way I would be joining them. If he had made them for four, then I would give him the benefit of the doubt.

I had trouble breathing as Janice dialed the number. I knew I was letting too much ride on this reservation, but ridiculously, I felt like my future was riding on the number Angus had given them. It would serve me right if he hadn't made any reservation at all, and here I was getting worked up about whether he had included me or not.

"Yes, hello," Janice said. "I was calling to check on a dinner reservation for tonight." She paused. "The last name is Barclay. I'm not sure if he made it under Dave or Angus." She paused again. "Oh good. Yes, seven-fifty is great. And how many do you have us down for? Yes, four is right. Thank you."

A little bubble of elation popped in my chest and warmed my insides.

It was a small thing, but Angus had made a

reservation for four.

"I'm going to head home and finish packing," I said. "And if we're going to Escape, I should probably change out of sweats."

"Come back whenever you're ready," Janice said.

"Or if you're busy, we can give you a call when we're leaving," Dave added.

My phone rang a little after six. It was Angus.

"Hi."

"Chuck. Sorry. Charles, I think I messed up." I smiled. Ever since the Chandlers had said I was too nice and too pretty to call Chuck, Angus had tried to avoid the nickname. I thought it was funny that he found Charles so much more acceptable, but hey, baby steps.

"You sure did."

"I forgot to tell you, didn't I?" He sounded contrite.

"Yes. But your parents told me, so you're off the hook. I even had time to come home and shower and change out of my sweats."

"I'm so sorry."

It often felt like I was on a teeter totter with Angus and today seemed to be teeter totter on steroids. He was sorry. He had meant to tell me.

"Don't worry about it. You're just lucky you made the reservation."

"Whew. At least I didn't forget that."

"And you're lucky you made it for four."

"What else would I have made it for?" I collapsed onto my bed and smiled. Teeter totter up. "Mom would have killed me if you couldn't come." Teeter totter down.

I sighed. How many times did I have to be put in my place and reminded that Angus wasn't budging on the whole "friend" thing? Of course it would have been his parents who insisted I be included.

"Don't let me forget," he said. "I've got a Christmas present for you." Teeter totter up.

"You do?"

"Yeah. I saw the Chandlers today and they asked me to make sure you got it."

"Oh." And teeter totter down. "How is Braxton?"

"He's doing well. I took a picture of him in his brace to show you. It's amazing how kids adapt. It looks like it should be difficult to walk in it, but he's cruising around the doctor's office like he was born with it."

He had taken a picture to show me. At least that was something.

"They're very grateful for what you did for him. So am I." Braxton had made forty-two of the rolled paper Christmas trees before he had been released from the hospital. That was enough for every hospital room on his floor that had patients, as well as both sets of grandparents and a few of the nurses and doctors. He had spent the last five days happy and entertained and feeling like he had a purpose. Before he left the hospital, his mom had pushed him around in a wheelchair to deliver the trees to the rooms close to his own.

"I loved helping him. He just needed somewhere to put his energy."

"Hey, Charles. I just got home. I'm going to go see Mom and Dad. You want to come down?"

"That's okay. I already saw them for a while. Just give me a call when we're leaving."

My bags were by the front door and the sheets were changed. I wore a belted navy sweater dress and boots. The boots weren't even warm, but at least they looked right for winter.

"This looks nice," Janice said when we arrived at Escape.

Andy saw us and made his way to the hostess stand.

"Charlotte. Couldn't stay away, could you?" He winked and pulled me into a hug as if we had been best friends. "Put them at one of my tables," he said to the hostess. "I'll take good care of you." He winked again.

I tried not to smirk. He was laying it on pretty thick.

"Does he have something in his eye?" Angus joked.

"Don't be jealous, dear," Janice said and I flushed.

"I'm not." Angus sounded a little defensive and I wanted to laugh. There was nothing for him to be jealous of, and I'm sure he knew that, even though Andy was cute.

We were almost through with our entrees when Boyd stepped up to the table. "I would imagine Andy's taking good care of you?"

"He's earning a nice tip," Dave said.

"How have you been, Charlotte?" he asked.

"Good. I'm working at Hallmark's Imaginarium."

"If you get tired of that, be sure to check back with us. We'd take you back."

"Thanks, Boyd. You're just saying that because your parmesan curls were a little weak tonight."

"I know, right?" He shook his head dramatically. "It's always hard to train the new help. She's trying hard, and I guess that's all we can ask. Please have dessert. On me." He put his hand over his heart. "And Merry Christmas."

"You made quite an impression on them," Angus said.

"That's why I always had enough to share."

Andy made his way to the table. "What can I get you for

dessert? Boyd's treat." He held up his hand like he was sharing a secret. "I could have sworn you weren't his type, Charlotte, but maybe I was wrong." He laughed at his little joke and took our orders.

When he returned with our desserts, I motioned him over. "Why are you being so stingy with the potato peeler trick?"

"Cause I'm not trying to impress her."

"Promise you'll show her before you leave tonight."

"Oh, all right."

"Can I trust you or should I go back and show her myself?"

Andy grinned. "I'll show her."

"Potato peeler?" Dave asked after Andy left the table.

"He taught me a trick for making the parmesan curls. He needs to teach the new girl."

"How long did you work here?" Angus asked.

"I was here twelve days."

"Looks like they'd have liked to keep you," Dave said.

"That's our Charlotte." Janice patted my hand. "This is delicious, by the way."

Everyone walked me home so Dave and Janice would know where my apartment was. I hugged them goodbye and then, because he was standing there with them and it would have been more awkward for us not to hug each other goodbye, Angus and I exchanged an uncomfortable and perfunctory embrace. I saw Dave and Janice exchange a look, but I couldn't worry about it. I had an early flight and I was going home to see my family. Tomorrow I would play with Emily and snuggle with Simon. Tomorrow night we would sing Christmas carols and read from the Bible and eat strawberry pancakes with chocolate macadamia sauce.

I had three weeks at home and I intended to enjoy every minute of it.

Chapter 21

Charlotte

There was something thrilling about being an out-of-town visitor at my family's home. Even though I hadn't lived with my parents for many years, I hadn't ever been treated like the honored guest until now. It made me glad I had moved to Kansas City even if nothing more ever happened with Angus.

I quickly shut off my brain, a skill I was getting quite proficient at. Even though Angus had given me no indication he would ever change his mind, and had in fact, placed me squarely in the friend zone, I refused to believe that a future with him was impossible. It was easier to shut down my mind when it started second-guessing my heart.

For more than a week, the family made every effort they could to come and spend time with me. Emily was charming, and after a few hours of hesitancy, decided her favorite game was loudly kissing my cheeks. McKayla was only allowed to hold Simon when he needed to be fed, since I had to soak up

157

all the baby time I could before I returned to Kansas City.

Two days after Christmas, I borrowed Mom's car and drove into the city for Mia's wedding.

"I hope you don't feel bad that I decided not to have any bridesmaids. If I would have, you'd have been one for sure."

"I don't feel bad at all. I feel nothing but happy for you. You both look wonderful."

And they did. Happiness was bouncing off them and onto everyone in the room. Mia's dress was simple and elegant. Her hair was in a twist with no veil and I was reminded of a conversation we'd had when we both wondered if we'd ever find love.

"I've even forgiven you for abandoning me," I said.

Mia raised an eyebrow. "Let's not forget who took off for the Midwest. *You* abandoned *me*."

"That's not what I meant," I explained. "Remember when you suggested we become stylish spinsters with a cat in the windowsill?"

Mia laughed. "That was still my plan for the future until you took off to Kansas City. How can we become spinster roommates when we don't even live in the same state?"

"I think Graham changed those plans, not me. At least you didn't give up on the stylish part. You look beautiful."

"Oh, Charlotte. I'd tell you your turn will come, but I remember how sick I got of hearing that, so I won't say it."

"Thank you."

"But I will say that if Angus is smart, he won't let you get away."

"And there's the one who made it happen." Graham put one arm around Mia and gave me a quick hug with his other arm.

I looked at him, surprised, and he laughed.

"Don't worry," Mia said. "He told me all about your

158

conversation at the airport. Thank you, by the way."

"I didn't do anything."

"You certainly did. You filled me with fear. I had visions of Mia marrying someone else. That was all it took."

I bowed. "I'm glad I could be of service."

"We might even name our firstborn Charlotte," Graham said.

"Or Charles," Mia added. "If it's a boy."

Mia's brother took the microphone and announced the bride and groom's first dance.

"I love you," Mia whispered in my ear as she hugged me again. Then Graham led her to the dance floor. A couple of minutes later, I left.

"Charlotte!" Ashley said when I stepped off the elevator at Jayne Fife.

I put my finger up to my lips to shush her. "I wanted to surprise Jayne. She's here, I hope."

Ashley put her finger to her lips in acknowledgement and nodded. "How are you?" she whispered.

"I'm good." I matched her tone. "How's your cute little boy?"

"Jax is great. He got his first bike for Christmas, so he's spent the last week trying to kill himself. Thank goodness for helmets." She motioned toward Jayne's office. "You'd better go see her before she catches us out here whispering."

I knocked on the frame of Jayne's door and she looked up, her expression changing from curiosity to excitement as soon as she saw me. She jumped up and met me just inside the door.

"I wondered if you were coming home for Christmas." She hugged me like an old friend instead of an employee. "It's a good thing you came by. You'd have been in big trouble if you hadn't stopped in to see me."

Jayne ushered me into her office and sat down. "Every time I see the weather in the Midwest, I think about you. You've had a lot of snow, haven't you?"

"We didn't have any until the week before Christmas and then it got a little crazy. I got snow boots and a parka for Christmas, but driving in it is pretty scary."

"Where are you working? I got a call from a guy at a temp agency asking about you."

I laughed. "Mark. Yeah. I did a couple of temporary jobs there. A restaurant and a big tractor company."

Jayne shook her head. "That's ridiculous. Why didn't you tell me? I could have assigned you another project from here."

"I thought about it. I don't know if it makes sense, but I wanted to find something there. The more I was tied to San Francisco, the easier it would be to give up and come home. I wanted to make it as hard on myself as possible." I shook my head. "I sound crazy, don't I?"

Jayne smiled. "A little. But I'm sure it's shown that boy of yours that you mean business." Jayne studied my rueful smile. "He does know you mean business, right?"

"I don't know what else I can do to get the point across, but so far he hasn't come around."

"You two aren't together?"

"We live in the same complex, and we see each other sometimes, but we're hardly together." I quickly continued when I saw Jayne's skeptical expression. "But he will. He'll come around. At least we're back to being friends."

Jayne looked worried. "Oh, Charlotte. I'm not sure what

to say. I thought this was going to be it for you, and I was so happy for you to be moving on after . . . you know . . . everything. You're sure you want to stick it out? Because I'm telling you right now, you've got a job here if you want to come back."

I didn't say anything right away. This was exactly the conversation I didn't want to have with people.

Will was the only one who knew for certain that Angus hadn't warmed back up to me, and thankfully, he hadn't set the record straight when the family talked about Angus and Kansas City. I had carefully skirted the whole Angus thing, focusing on my job and my apartment and the time Angus and I had spent together. It wasn't difficult to make it sound like everything was going well, especially since that was what everyone expected. Dad had even asked when I thought Angus might call to have a talk with him and I had coyly shrugged it off. I had surprised myself at how duplicitous I was capable of being. Will had even teased me about a career change.

"Too bad Angus didn't go to Hollywood," he had whispered, sitting next to me at dinner. "You could have pursued a career in acting."

I elbowed him. "Oh, shut up."

"This might be good enough for an Oscar."

"It's not acting. It's positive thinking."

"Oh, that's what we're calling it." Will smiled, and I knew my secret was safe with him. For a while, anyway.

Now I had told Jayne the truth, and I was already second-guessing myself. I didn't want any suggestions that I should give up and come home.

Like the suggestion Jayne was making now. "We can always use you around here, you know." Jayne grinned mischievously. "I'd be especially happy to have you here over the next year or so."

"Why the next year?"

Jayne stood and turned sideways, pulling her stylish, sweater tight over the little bump in her abdomen. She patted her stomach. "I'll be taking a little time off and I'd love to have you around to help keep things in order here."

"Oh, my goodness. I'm so happy for you," I said as I made my way around the desk to give her a hug.

Jayne smiled. "We're pretty happy, too."

We talked about the baby's sex (boy), name options (Bard, after Shakespeare or Darby, after some 1980s singer. Yikes! I kept my opinions on those to myself), Jayne's due date (July) and the chances of me coming back (it depended on Angus, but hopefully small).

A strange thing happened to me after I left Jayne Fife Graphics. For the first time since I had decided to follow Angus to Kansas City, I let myself think about what it would be like to come back.

It wasn't all bad.

"I'm sorry I won't be here tonight," Gina said as she zipped her boots over her jeans. I marveled at how she could wear such high heels. It was a talent I'd never needed to acquire. "But it'll be nice for you and Will to catch up. And Emily will be in heaven, won't you, sweet pea." She nuzzled Emily's neck until she started giggling.

"Have fun with your sister," Will said. "I'll try not to let Charles kidnap your firstborn."

"What shall we get for dinner," Will asked after Gina left.

"I was hoping you'd feel like eating at The Mouse Trap. I haven't had a good cheese sandwich in months."

We talked about Will's cases over gooey cheese sandwiches. Mine had apples and cheddar and a brown sugar glaze. It was messy and wonderful. Emily finished an entire sandwich by herself and even had a bite of mine.

It was quiet when we returned to Will's. I sat cross-legged in the corner of the couch, holding Emily on my lap as she looked at a book. Will sat in the other corner, his legs stretched out on the coffee table.

"Now you're all fed and happy, tell me how you're really doing." I could tell from Will's serious expression he didn't want the sugar-coated, convince-everyone-things-are-great version.

"I don't know."

"Yes, you do. Dig deep, Chuck, and tell me how you're feeling about everything."

I smiled. "Angus is trying not to call me Chuck anymore. One of Angus's patients told him I was too nice to be called Chuck. He still slips sometimes, but he's doing better."

"Traitor."

"You should stop using that ugly nickname, too, you know."

"That'll never happen."

"I figured."

"Is he nice to you?" Will asked.

I shrugged. I thought carefully as I talked, wanting to be as truthful with Will as possible. If there was one person in the world who could help me sort out this mess, it was probably Will. He loved us both and he could be brutally honest. It was a combination I needed.

"I guess so. He keeps telling me to move back here, which

is annoying, but it's not really mean. He's super busy so he doesn't have a lot of time. But if he wanted to, he could make time. Sometimes I wonder if he keeps his distance to try to get me to come home." I stroked Emily's soft curls. "Other times I think maybe I was just wrong."

"Wrong about what?"

"Wrong about how he feels. About me. Like maybe when he kissed me and told me he loved me, he was confused and he didn't really mean it. Or maybe he thought he did and now he realizes he was wrong and he wishes I'd leave him alone."

I was glad it wasn't too light—just a couple of lamps— because a tear slid down my cheek and landed in Emily's hair. I rested my cheek on her head and she didn't pull away.

Will clasped his hands behind his head and stared across the room. He didn't say anything right away and I let him think, hoping he would have some insight when he finally spoke. "Charles, I don't have any idea what he's thinking anymore. Maybe he really is over you and wants to move on. But I can tell you this for sure. He did love you. He loved you for a long time."

"Why didn't anyone tell me?"

"We should have. Gina told me I should tell you, especially after Kyle, but I thought you two would figure things out." He slapped my knee. "I didn't know you were both so incompetent."

"How was I so stupid? I think back over the years and I can't believe how clueless I was. Did I really think he was going to therapy and hanging out with me all those years because we were friends?"

"Don't write off the friend thing too much, Charles. You two were friends. He wanted more, but you've always been friends. That didn't change."

I felt sad. "I might have ruined it."

"If it's ruined, you didn't do it by yourself." Will sat up and put his feet on the floor. "Look, Angus is a good man. And he's a smart guy. I can't imagine him wanting to lose your friendship. I think that's why it took him so long to fess up and tell you. I can't help but think he's going to come around and stop holding a grudge."

Emily was almost asleep. I closed the book and put it on the table and talked a little quieter. "How long do I wait?"

"I don't know."

"Jayne offered me my job back today. I miss it there."

"I thought you liked your job at Hallmark."

"I do. The kids are great. Mostly." We both smiled. "But it's not designing. It's like babysitting with crafts. Except when I taught Braxton. That felt like it mattered. Like I was doing something important."

"Maybe they'll have a design job open soon." Will leaned forward, his elbows on his knees. "Or maybe you should come back to your job here."

"Do you really think that?"

"I don't know, Charles. I have a feeling if you're patient, Angus will come around. But what if I'm wrong? What if I feel that way because I want that to happen? I'd feel sick if you put in all this time and he didn't come around and you lost out on your job because I'd encouraged you to stay."

I straightened one of my legs and kicked him. "You're a lot of help."

"Yeah? Well, I didn't ask for the job of Angus and Charlotte's therapist. You two were supposed to be taking care of that on your own."

"We're hopeless."

"I don't know about that."

Will stood and reached for Emily. "I'll put her to bed."

As soon as she was out of my arms, she squirmed with sleepy eyes and reached for me. "Shuck. Shuck."

"And this is why you should have stopped calling me Chuck a long time ago."

Will laughed and handed her back to me. She snuggled in and closed her eyes. "I guess someone loves you," Will said.

"Thank you, Emily." I kissed her forehead.

Chapter 22

Angus

I stared at the rolled paper Christmas tree on the door of the refrigerator. Even though it said "Love Braxton" at the bottom of the paper, it hadn't made me think of my little patient. It made me think of Chuck. I mean Charles. I groaned and opened the door to get the milk.

It made me think of Charlotte.

"What's the matter?" Mom sat at the counter eating a piece of toast. Dad was showering after a morning workout at the clubhouse.

"Just having a bowl of cereal." I poured milk into the bowl.

"Do you always groan when you have a bowl of cereal?"

I laughed. "Only when I'm working through problems." I sat down at the counter beside her.

"Problems you can share? I can tell something's been on your mind since we got here. Maybe it would help to

167

talk about it."

"There's nothing to talk about."

Mom finished a bite of toast. "Are things okay with your residency?"

"They're fine. I like the doctors I'm working with. Maybe not quite as much as Dr. Fickland, but they've all been very nice."

"Are you wishing you hadn't come?"

"Not at all. The fellowship is a big deal. It's good I'm here." I took another bite of cereal, wishing Mom would be satisfied talking about the weather or politics. Maybe I could steer the conversation. "Are you and Dad still wanting to go to the Mennonite store tomorrow?"

"I'd like to. That quilt auction sounds fun, although I'm not sure why they wouldn't have tried to sell their quilts before Christmas. Maybe we can find a little gift for Charlotte to thank her for letting us stay in her apartment."

Dad had been looking online for activities and had found a Mennonite store about fifty miles outside the city. The store itself looked interesting, but tomorrow they were auctioning off some of their handmade quilts.

"The weather looks good, so the drive shouldn't be a problem," I said.

"I don't mind the drive. And maybe if we have you trapped in the car long enough, you'll finally tell your dad and me what's going on with you." Mom smiled to let me know she wasn't fooled by my attempt at a subject change.

I sighed and shook my head. "You think you're smart, don't you?" She shrugged and took a sip of her orange juice. "Fine. It's Charlotte."

"Charlotte? Who's that?"

We laughed.

"I don't think I've ever heard you call her Charlotte. It's

always been Charles or Chuck or Charlie. Poor girl. What about Charlotte?"

"I want her to move back home. She shouldn't be here."

Mom nodded but waited for me to continue.

"I didn't even know she was coming until she was here. She left a good job. She left her family. I can tell she misses them. She should just go back home. But she's so stubborn, she won't listen to me. Every time I bring it up, she shuts down or takes off. Mom, she left a dream job to babysit."

"And you feel guilty?" Mom asked.

"I guess. But I didn't ask her to come." I pushed my stool back and put my dish in the sink a little rougher than necessary. "The main reason I came was to get away from her."

"That's what you want?" Mom looked genuinely innocent. "To be away from her?"

"How am I supposed to move on if I have to worry about her?"

I felt defeated. I leaned against the counter and dug my hands through my hair.

Mom's voice was calm when she spoke. "Has she asked you to worry about her?"

"No. But if she's here with no one but me, how can I help it?"

Mom was quiet for a moment. "Angus, can I ask you a hard question without you getting upset?"

I had no interest in answering any questions, but I was curious where she was going.

"Sure."

"For years you've dated girls but never really given them a chance."

"That's not . . ."

Mom put her hand up to stop me. "Now let me finish before you say anything. You've dated a lot of pretty, smart, charming girls. But you've never let them in. You've never let it go past a certain point. I've always thought it was because you were holding out for Charlotte, but maybe I've been wrong."

"You weren't wrong," I admitted.

"Then why? Why when you finally have the girl you've been waiting for right there, ready to sacrifice everything for you, why are you turning your back on her?"

I should have told her I wasn't taking questions. But since she had asked, I'd tell her.

"She left me hanging for years. And now, just because nothing else has worked out, I'm supposed to be ready to jump right in? She's my friend. Her whole family are my friends. What happens when things don't work out? Then I've lost them all. It's not worth it."

Mom nodded. "You're right. There's a lot at stake. I can see how you wouldn't want to lose the Emersons."

I turned to see if she was messing with me, but she looked sincere.

"Thank you, Mom." She smiled at me, and I felt like finally someone got it.

"I never understood what happened with you two," she said.

"I got carried away and told her I was in love with her."

"And so she followed you?"

"First she followed that guy to Scotland."

"Oh. That must have been hard."

I sat down beside Mom and clasped my hands on the counter. It felt good to finally tell her what I had gone through the past year.

"It was. But now I realize it was probably a good thing."

"That she went to Scotland?"

I nodded. "It let me know things would never be what I'd wanted them to be. It reminded me what I'd be losing if I wasn't careful."

"The Emersons."

"Yeah. It made it clear I needed to move on."

"And have you? Moved on, I mean."

Mom's face held nothing but love and concern. "It's why I came to Kansas City. It's why I want Charles to go home."

Mom reached over and patted my hand. "Angus, have you ever pictured the future if you marry another woman?"

I shrugged.

"Perhaps you should."

"What do you mean?"

"How will another woman fit in with your life? Will you still be close to the Emersons? How will it be to watch Charlotte marry someone else? Will you still feel comfortable at birthday parties if you're there with someone else and Charlotte's there with another man and their children? I think you need to play out every scenario in your mind as you're deciding your future. If none of those things will be difficult, then maybe you were never really in love with her. If it sounds horribly awkward and uncomfortable, maybe you'll choose not to stay close with the Emersons anyway. Just look at every angle and follow it to its conclusion. It might help you see things more clearly."

"You think Charlotte and I should be together?"

"I'm not saying that at all. You need to do what's right for you."

Mom stood and hugged me from behind, kissing my cheek before she straightened.

"My only advice would be not to give her false hope if

171

you really aren't in love with her."

"I'm not," I lied. "I've told her over and over that I think she should go home."

"And then you shared her dinner and had Thanksgiving together and asked her to help you with a patient." Mom ruffled my hair like I was a toddler. "I'm going to go see what on earth is taking your father so long. Have a good day at work, honey. We'll see you when you get home."

Mom picked up her keys and left for Chuck's apartment—I mean Charlotte's apartment—like she hadn't just detonated a grenade in my life.

No. Not Charlotte's apartment.

"Chuck. Chuck. Chuck. Chuck. Chuck." I felt much better.

"Sold, to the man in the blue scarf." The bearded auctioneer pointed at my dad.

This was the second quilt Dad had bought in the last hour. The first had been what they called a Cathedral Window quilt that Mom had fallen in love with. This was a small quilt, more like a throw. The auctioneer had called it a Log Cabin quilt, although I couldn't see anything about it that looked like a log cabin. Maybe it was called that because it would look good in a mountain retreat, but that could be said about every quilt, couldn't it?

"You're sure she'll like it?" Dad asked. He was talking about Charles since they'd purchased it to leave as a gift for her.

"She'll love it," Mom and I said in unison.

"I think we should go pay for this and then look through

the store before we're tempted to buy another quilt." Mom stood and scooted in front of the people sitting on the folding chairs in the barn.

"Or before we freeze to death," I said to Dad.

The Mennonite store was the front part of a barn. The quilt auction had taken place in the back. I don't think they had ever kept animals in here because the overriding smell was sawdust. People around us were wrapped up in blankets. They must have known there was no heat. Mom was freezing and my nose and fingers were cold. Maybe it was a calculated move to make buying a quilt feel like a survival tactic instead of just a regular purchase.

The little storefront was warmed by a potbelly stove in the middle of the room. The aisles were filled with bags of homemade soup mixes and pastas, nuts and candies, and spices. Mom insisted on getting Charlotte a bag of chocolate covered cashews and me a few groceries even though I protested that I couldn't do much cooking. It turned out to be an expensive adventure, but neither of them complained.

I pulled off the gravel road that led to the Mennonite store and onto the paved road leading back to the city. Deep snow covered the fields on either side of us, but the roads were clear.

"I've heard it's beautiful here in the summer," Dad said. "Lots of flowers and green rolling hills."

"It was pretty when I got here. But I've heard the summers are hot and humid."

"Maybe we should come visit again in the spring or fall." Mom didn't like humidity. Her grandparents had lived in South Carolina and every time Mom had visited them, the heat had made her sick.

"I think I'll be able to come home for a week or so

this summer," I said.

"Good. I don't like having you so far away." Mom stared out the window and I wondered if she was crying. She wiped at her cheeks and confirmed my suspicion. "And you'd better take a job close to home once you're finished. I want to know my grandkids." Dad reached up and squeezed Mom's shoulder.

"I'm sure he'll do his best, honey." Mom put her hand over Dad's. "Speaking of grandchildren . . ." Dad continued.

I laughed. "I know. I know. You don't have any."

"But we'd like to. Your mom will make a wonderful grandmother."

"Are you purposely ganging up on me?" I asked Mom.

She shook her head. "I didn't even tell Dad about our talk yesterday."

"What did I miss out on?" Dad asked.

"Mom thinks I should think through my future life with and without Charles."

"Charlotte," Mom said good-naturedly.

"Chuck," I said and we laughed.

"It's good advice," Dad said.

"I know it is." I glanced at Dad in the rearview mirror. I recognized his expression. I'd seen it throughout my life whenever he had something he wanted to tell me. He was measuring his words carefully. "You can say whatever you have to say, Dad."

He smiled. "And you'll listen?"

"You've got me trapped in a car. Do I have any choice?"

"I guess not."

Dad took a minute. When he finally spoke, I was surprised at what he had to say.

"I hate to see you become a gambling man."

"What?" I'd never had an interest in gambling so I wasn't

sure what he was talking about.

"If a man goes to a casino, he'd better be willing to do without whatever he puts on that table because most likely he's going to lose it. You should never gamble with something you're not ready to live without."

No one said anything for several miles. Dad didn't need to finish his thought and he knew it. We all knew it.

I was gambling with Charlotte, and I had to make a decision.

I'd tried so hard to convince myself that I was willing to live without Charlotte, but was I really?

I sat on the couch in my pajama bottoms and a t-shirt. It was my first day off since Dad and Mom had returned to San Francisco, and I felt a little lost. Through the window the world was foggy and gray, perfectly matching my state of mind.

I closed the medical journal and tossed it to the other side of the couch. There was no point in finishing the article Dr. Winters had suggested right now. Nothing was sticking anyway and I knew I'd end up reading it again later. I ran my hands over my stubbly chin and then clasped them behind my head, staring out at the milky morning.

My apartment was too quiet. The teapot-shaped clock on the kitchen wall behind me ticked off the seconds.

Tick.

Tick.

Tick.

It had to be slow. Seconds didn't really stretch out

that long.

I missed Dad and Mom. Was a twenty-eight year-old man supposed to miss his parents this much? Probably not. But right now I didn't much want to be twenty-eight. I wanted to be young enough that Mom could tell me what to do or Dad could call me into the living room for a talk—the kind of talk that took all my confusion and put things in order, making my next move clear.

I'd had one of those talks when I was trying to decide what to study in school. Dad never told me what to do, he just asked all the right questions and when we were through talking, I had known I wanted to go to medical school.

I thought over the conversations I'd had while Mom and Dad were here. Dad had told me not to gamble with Charlotte unless I was prepared to lose her. Mom had said to look at my options and follow them to their conclusions.

I kept talking about moving on with my life, but that meant finding another woman to date. It meant not breaking up with her when things started getting serious. It meant commitment and eventually marriage and a family. Did I really want to move on with my life? Did I want to take those steps with someone who wasn't Charlotte?

No. I didn't.

The force of what I'd been doing hit me like a Randy Johnson pitch to the head. I had been pushing away the thing I had wanted most for the past eight years. Loving Charlotte didn't mean risking my friendship with her and her family. Not loving her was the greater gamble.

I didn't want a future with some nameless, faceless woman.

I just wanted Charlotte.

Chapter 23

Charlotte

The freeway was a parking lot. I wondered if it was a sign that I shouldn't be going. Maybe Angus was right. If I had listened to him, I'd be at Mom and Dad's house enjoying one of my last evenings at home. Instead, I was stuck on the freeway, alone, and second-guessing my strange determination to attend the weddings of my ex-boyfriends.

I turned on the radio, hoping I could find out what the hold-up was and how long it would last. After about ten minutes of commercials and weather, and ironically a story about Senator Aldsworth, a traffic update let me know there was a four-car pileup at the end of the bridge. Emergency crews were clearing the scene and traffic would be moving again in the next half hour.

Annoyed by the chattering of the DJ, I scanned through the channels trying to find a decent song. Eventually I gave up, turned off the radio, and settled in to wait it out.

The clock in the car said six-eleven. Kyle and Wyatt were

probably standing in the rotunda of the San Francisco City Hall, exchanging their vows. City Hall was a perfect venue for them. It was large enough to hold a few thousand guests, and the architecture was perfect for getting good pictures. Plus it provided a measure of civic loyalty and political clout. I wondered if Devon and Polly had helped select the site.

I wondered what they'd look like. Would Kyle's hair be a little longer and wavier, the way it had been when we were dating? Or would it be shorter like it had been when he'd come to see me last spring? What kind of dress would Wyatt have chosen? Whatever it was, I knew it would be beautiful. Wyatt had impeccable taste. I fluffed the skirt of the navy chiffon dress McKayla had helped me find a few days earlier. It was a beautiful dress, but how would it compare with the finery of the other guests? This would certainly be the most extravagant wedding I'd ever attended.

Too bad Angus wasn't in town to come with me.

But if Angus were here, he probably would have talked me out of going.

I didn't want to think about Angus right now. Every time I thought of him, my future stretched out in front of me, hazy and uncertain. Was it a good idea to give up so much to be with him? He didn't want me there. Was I making a fool of myself? Jayne had offered me my job. What if Angus never came around and I had given up my dream job not once, but twice? I didn't want to give up, but at what point was it better for me to cut my losses and move on?

The lane of cars on both sides of me began inching forward but my lane didn't move. It was a cruel metaphor for my life. A couple of minutes later, my lane moved a car length. And then another. I should have been happy to finally be making progress, but instead, a feeling of dread settled on me. I had never gone to an ex-boyfriend's wedding before without

Angus being around for post-wedding therapy. Why hadn't I realized that before I bought a dress and drove into the city?

Despite the anxiety I felt, I kept on course and forty minutes later, a valet took my car and I walked in the front doors of City Hall.

I was standing beside a podium set up inside the front doors, showing my invitation to a large man in a suit, when I heard my name. "Charlotte, is that you?"

I turned to see who it was.

"Roberta. Hello."

"It is you. How are you, dear?"

Roberta Aldsworth looked stunning in a taupe lace skirt and silk jacket. She took my hands in hers and kissed me on the cheek. Not the over-the-shoulder air kiss I was expecting. Her lips actually touched my skin.

"I'm sorry." I don't know if she had actually left lipstick there, but she swiped it with her thumb and then briefly put both hands on my cheeks. "I'm just so happy to see you."

Roberta stepped back and looked me up and down. "You look lovely."

"Thank you. So do you. I'm sorry I missed the wedding. There was an accident on the bridge. I sat there for more than an hour."

"You poor thing. The wedding was lovely." Roberta looked at her watch and then linked her arm through mine and guided me to a beautiful table at the edge of the room. "I didn't think we'd see you tonight. Kyle said something about you moving to Scotland."

"Oh, no. That was a vacation. I didn't move there. But I have moved to Kansas City."

"What took you to Kansas City?"

"A friend of mine moved there, and I was ready for a change. I'm working for Hallmark."

"Of course you are."

The room was crowded with beautiful people in beautiful clothes. It was even more impressive than the Mercy House benefit had been. I craned my neck, trying to catch a glimpse of the bride and groom.

Roberta noticed and said, "They're with the photographer getting a few pictures. They'll be back in soon."

I admired the table where we sat. It was one of dozens of tables covered with silver and crystal and blush-colored ranunculus. Of course it was as resplendent as I had expected it to be.

"Everything is lovely," I said. "Of course, I expected it to be with you and Wyatt involved."

"She did most of it. She's a talented young woman." Roberta didn't seem eager to leave, but I glanced around to see if anyone had noticed that I was monopolizing the mother of the groom. I felt a little of the anxiousness that had been my constant companion after the reporter had lied and twisted my words. This world of the Aldsworths had felt so perilous.

"Charlotte, tell me how you've been."

I started to speak, but a chant calling for Kyle and Wyatt had started on the other side of the room. "You should go," I said quickly. "I'd hate for you to miss their entrance."

We stood and looked the direction of the voices. Roberta stopped and turned back to me. "I've wanted to tell you how much I admire you, Charlotte. You're a beautiful and unselfish young woman and I'm honored to have had the chance to know you."

I wanted to thank her, but my throat tightened and I didn't trust myself to speak.

"I hope you find more happiness than you can hold," she continued and pulled me into another hug. "It was wonderful of you to come."

"Roberta?" She paused and turned back to me. "Thank you for being so kind to me."

She smiled. "It was easy."

I watched Kyle's mother gracefully weave her way through the guests to be at the front of the room. She leaned over and whispered something in Donald's ear, and he smiled down at her. I couldn't see all of Kyle's brothers, but Alex was standing at the bottom of the stairs with a curvy blonde.

I stood by the table and watched as Kyle and Wyatt appeared at the top of the wide stairway. Guests cheered as they joyfully raised their held hands in the air, smiles on their faces.

Of course it was all fit for royalty. Kyle was handsome and Wyatt was gorgeous. The tuxedo was impeccable and the skirt of the bias-cut dress draped gracefully over the top three or four stairs, making Wyatt look impossibly tall and elegant. Thousands of beads made the dress sparkle, even from the back of the room. The immense room twinkled and glowed beneath them. I couldn't help but picture how different my wedding would be—a small chapel, my groom in a well-cut suit, me in a simple dress. The only thing sparkling would be the stained glass sending liquid color onto the floor around us. The crowd of thousands would be replaced with just our families and a few close friends.

Kyle and Wyatt shared a passionate kiss as their loyal subjects cheered, and then they started down the stairs.

And then a strange thing happened. Suddenly I didn't

know why I was here. I thought about myself at all the other weddings I had attended and wondered why I had felt the need to be there. What had been the strange compulsion that had driven me to attend every wedding I had been invited to? Had I wanted to see the discomfort on the grooms' faces? Had I wanted to see the evidence that they knew I'd been slighted? Did I want them to know I forgave them so they'd be grateful and realize they shouldn't have let me slip away?

All those times I had thought I was attending their weddings for them. Now I realized it had probably been for me, so I could feel the sting of betrayal one last time before I closed the chapter. It was crazy. No wonder Angus wanted me to stay away. He hadn't wanted me to suffer any more.

Kyle and Wyatt were no longer on the stairs. I wasn't sure where they were, but it no longer mattered. I turned and walked back the way I had come. I handed my valet ticket to the man at the podium who called for my car.

I felt good. I didn't need to see Kyle and Wyatt. I didn't need to congratulate them or put their minds at ease. I didn't need any apologies or sympathetic looks. I didn't feel sad or slighted or hurt. I felt buoyant and optimistic and happy.

I wished Angus was here, but not because I wanted or needed our usual therapy session. That wasn't it at all.

I just wanted Angus.

My phone vibrated in my pocket. It was Will.

"I just pulled up your flight information and it says you haven't left the airport yet."

I looked out the tiny airplane window at the blue, San Francisco sky. "Nope. We're still sitting here on the runway.

They've delayed our flight by an hour. Something about a storm in Kansas City that I guess we're trying to miss."

"And they're not letting you off the plane?"

A baby howled a few rows back and I felt sorry for the parents. "No. Everyone's getting a little antsy."

"I guess antsy is better than a stormy plane crash."

"Thank you, Will. I love hearing the words 'stormy plane crash' when I'm sitting on the runway waiting to take off into stormy weather."

"Sorry, sis. But it's true. I'd rather you wait there than be thrown around in the turbulence caused by gale-force winds that ripped part of one of the wings off and disrupted the balance of the plane, sending it into a spin that required an emergency crash landing somewhere high in the Rocky Mountains, where rescue is difficult and the passengers that live have to feed on their dearly departed flight companions in order to survive."

I laughed. "You're a sick man, William Emerson."

"I know. How soon are you taking off?"

"Pretty soon, I think."

"Have they told you what time you'll be landing in Kansas City?"

"No, but we're an hour late taking off so I imagine we'll be an hour late landing."

"That's if you take off on time. Would you let me know? Call me or text me."

"Um, why are you so interested in my flight?" His curiosity seemed excessive.

"Why wouldn't I be? My wonderful sister is on board that flight."

"Oh, brother."

"I just want to let Mom know. She always worries."

That made sense. "Tell her we're fine and I'll call her when I land."

"Love ya, Chuck. It was good to see you."

I smiled when I tapped the end button. A crew of baggage handlers were loading an airplane not far away. They had a portable conveyer belt that moved large bags right into the belly of the giant plane. Were they going somewhere warm? If so, I wanted to switch flights. Even though I was now the proud owner of moon boots and a parka, I wasn't excited to go back to snow and winter weather.

"Ladies and gentleman, this is your captain. I'm terribly sorry for the inconvenience, but we're going to be holding tight another forty minutes or so which will, of course, affect our arrival time in Kansas City. Please see one of our flight attendants if you have a question about connecting flights out of Kansas City. Here at Skyways Airlines, we're committed to providing you with a quality flying experience. Please remain seated while we continue to prepare for takeoff."

I texted Will.

Me: Another forty minute delay. This is fun!

Will: Glad it's you and not me. Keep us posted.

Forty minutes came and went, and with every passing minute, the cabin became more restless. It had been more than an hour since the captain's last announcement.

Me: I'm afraid they might have a riot on their hands if they don't take off or let us off the plane.

Will: You haven't left yet?

Me: Nope. Just sitting here relaxing with my knees near my chin.

Will would understand the discomfort an airplane seat

posed for tall people.

Will: Maybe you should get off and find another flight.

Me: It's tempting.

Will: Let me know when you finally take off.

Almost two and a half hours after our scheduled departure time, the captain announced we were ready to take off.

Me: I've got to turn my phone off. The captain says we're ready to roll.

Will: Be safe. Love you.

I rested my head against the side of the plane and watched California disappear until I fell asleep.

My screaming, pretzeled legs woke me up a couple of hours later. I knew if I didn't get up and stretch them I might not be able to walk when we landed, so I reluctantly disturbed the two people between me and the aisle and made my way to the cramped restroom. I flexed and stretched my legs as I waited my turn. I felt considerably better when I returned to my seat.

Darkness had settled on the world while I had slept, and with it a cloud of uneasiness. Despite living there for more than two months, I still didn't really know Kansas City. It was one thing to take a cab to my apartment in the daylight. A cab ride in the dark made me a little apprehensive.

"Ladies and gentleman, this is Captain Van Ness. Because of today's bad weather, air traffic is a bit backed up. We'll be circling the greater Kansas City area while we await our turn to land. Don't worry. This should be a minor delay, and we're in no danger of running low on fuel." He chuckled a little before he continued. "Please remain seated with your seatbelts fastened. Thank you."

The groans and grumbling started before he finished. I'm pretty sure he wouldn't have laughed if he'd known how unhappy most of the passengers were.

I don't know how long we circled the city. My phone was in my bag, conveniently stowed beneath the seat in front of me. The man in the seat behind me counted our rotations. Every time we passed over Arrowhead Stadium, he added a number. He made it to five before we began our descent.

A freezing draft blew through the jet bridge. I shivered. I would need to get my parka out of my suitcase before I went out to call a taxi.

We moved as a slow, tired herd toward the escalators that would lead us to the luggage carousels. In front of me, a woman tried to wrangle in her three children who were releasing the energy they'd had to keep in check for the last seven hours.

I stepped on the escalator and let my eyes wander over the room. There were hugs and squeals of delight as loved ones greeted each other.

A couple of people, obviously drivers, held signs with names on them. One said Spears, and I wondered if I had just flown with Britney Spears. Not likely.

A tall man held a sign that said, "My Girlfriend." Ah, that was cute in a cheesy, awkward sort of way. Lucky girl.

And then I looked at his face. It was Angus and he was smiling. At me.

I'm not sure what my face did, but it must not have been pretty, because Angus laughed.

I stopped when I reached the bottom of the escalator. A couple of people bumped into me and then a man with an unpleasant voice said, "Hey lady, get out of the way, would ya?"

I moved out of the way, my eyes not leaving Angus. I couldn't read the sign anymore because he was holding out his arms and walking to meet me.

And then Angus pulled me into his arms.

It could have been a dream, except that if I had been dreaming, my bag would have magically disappeared instead of the corner painfully jabbing me in the ribs. It must have been poking Angus, too, because he leaned away, moved the bag around to my back, and then pulled me back into his arms.

He smelled a little like surgery in an Indian restaurant by the beach on a rainy day. It was wonderful and I never wanted to smell anything else.

"What are you doing here?" I asked.

"Giving you a ride home."

I pulled back a little. "Why? I was planning to take a cab."

"Isn't this what good boyfriends do?" His arms were still around my waist as I studied his face.

The crowd had moved on and we were as alone as we would ever be in a large international airport.

"Angus, what are you saying?" I whispered.

"That I'm sorry." He pulled me close again, and his lips met mine in the sweetest kiss I'd ever had. It didn't matter that we were at an airport. It didn't matter that there were still a few people passing by us. The kiss was slow and warm and gentle. "We should go get your bags." he said when our lips finally parted. He hugged me again, his cheek against mine.

"There's only one." I picked up the hand-written sign that had fallen to the floor and tucked it under my arm. We held hands as we walked slowly to the luggage carousel. My suitcase looked lonely and neglected as it circled its way toward us.

Angus didn't let go of my hand as he lugged it off the

conveyor. We walked in silence through the airport and out into the dark, cold air. We boarded a shuttle, the bright, artificial lights harsh and jarring. I glanced at Angus and found him smiling at me. He pulled me close and kissed my cheek before he rested his head against mine.

I didn't want to talk. I was afraid to. What if I broke this fragile spell and Angus sternly told me I should get back on the plane and go home?

"We get off here," Angus said at the third stop. The car wasn't far from the drop off and Angus opened my door and then threw my bag into the back seat. "Sorry the car's so cold," he said as he turned up the heat and adjusted the vents. "It's been sitting out here for hours."

"You've been here a long time?"

"I didn't dare leave. I was afraid I'd miss you. Will let me know your flight had been delayed."

I smiled. "Will knows about this?"

"I had to have someone tell me your plans."

No wonder Will had been so interested in when the plane finally took off.

Angus turned in his seat, rubbed his hands together to warm them, and then took my hands in his. He looked at our hands when he started to speak.

"I've been an idiot and I'm sorry. You gave me a huge gift when you came out here, and I was afraid if I accepted it, I'd be setting myself up for disappointment or you'd end up hating me for making you leave everything behind. If we messed things up, we'd lose our friendship forever. But that's like saying I'd rather hang on tight and be satisfied with a piece of chocolate chip pie instead of letting go and having the whole bakery."

I started laughing. "Thank you for making it relatable for me. You probably wanted to say you were hanging on tight to the barbecued rib when you wanted the whole pig farm."

Angus laughed. "See? We get each other. Why would we want to look for someone else?"

I hadn't known I was going to cry, but a tear made a surprise escape down my cheek, and I couldn't stand not kissing him a moment longer. I took his face in both my hands and kissed him the way I had wanted to when I came home from Scotland, the way I'd wanted to when I came to Kansas City.

Angus pulled me close, his arm around my waist. It was so different than any of our other kisses. Aleena wasn't waiting for Angus in the yard. I wasn't trying to convince Angus to stay in San Francisco. There was no desperation or confusion, only confidence and trust. Years of longing and hope and friendship and love came together in one long, perfect kiss.

My phone started chirping.

Angus groaned against my mouth. "They're probably wondering if you landed safely."

Angus backed out of the parking place while I answered Will's call.

"Hi, Will. I'm here."

"Good. Any news?"

"Let's see, is there any news?" Angus squeezed my hand. "I don't ever want to fly again if there's bad weather. That was a nightmare. We circled Kansas City five times."

"That must have been rough."

"It's really cold here. The captain said the current temperature in Kansas City is three degrees. I don't think I've ever been somewhere this cold before. The cab driver must be wearing three coats." Angus grinned.

"Cab driver?" Will sounded confused.

"How did you think I was getting home?" I asked.

"Right. Yeah. A cab. I guess I just hadn't thought it through."

I laughed. "Angus says hi, Will."

Will laughed, too. "All right. You got me. Were you surprised?"

"Shocked."

"Which sign did he decide to use?"

"There were different signs?" I looked at Angus. He smiled and shrugged.

"Uh, oh. Maybe I wasn't supposed to say that."

"I'll show you when we get home," Angus said.

Will's voice got quiet. "Gina wants to know if you're glad you went back."

"Very."

"She's glad," he said to Gina.

"Good," I heard Gina say. "Tell her we love her. Tell them both."

"We both love you," Will said.

"You know what I meant," Gina said, laughing.

"We love you both. Talk to you soon."

Even though my parking place was covered, wind had drifted snow so high, my car was almost unrecognizable.

"I'll help you dig that out in the morning," Angus said. He drove around the lot to his parking place. He picked up several pieces of cardstock from the back seat when he pulled out my suitcase. I gave him a questioning look and he held them up. "My sign options."

The cold bit into my skin and burned my eyes as we walked up the flight of stairs to my apartment.

"I used the key you left my parents and turned the heat up before I came to get you," Angus said. I was glad. The apartment felt warm and cozy, the way home should feel.

I took off my coat and put it on the back of one of the stools. "I can head home if you're tired," Angus said.

"No way are you heading home yet. I want to see those signs."

Angus took off his coat and put it on the back of the other stool. I pulled him to the living room and we sat down, facing each other.

"Don't let these freak you out," he said.

"I'm not going to freak out."

"Don't be too sure. You haven't seen them yet. Let me explain what I was thinking."

Angus held up the first sign. It read "Charlotte."

"Ooh." I pretended to tremble. "I can see what you mean. That's pretty freaky."

"This should make you happy. I didn't write Chuck or Charles or even Charlie."

I nodded seriously. "I do appreciate that."

Angus held up the second sign. It was the one he had held at the airport. "My girlfriend."

"I almost didn't use this one," he said.

"Why?"

He shrugged. "Girlfriend sounds like we're seventeen or something. It's such a cheesy word."

"I love cheese." I leaned forward and kissed him on the mouth. "And I love this sign. Can I keep it?"

"I don't need it."

"Can I keep all of them?"

"You might not want the last one."

"Why not?"

"Because this is the one I was afraid might freak you out." He held it close to his chest. "In some ways it felt like this one would be okay because we already know practically everything about each other. But in another way, it seemed like it might be assuming a lot, considering our history." With every word, my heart raced faster. "That's why I didn't use it, even though I seriously thought about it. I don't want to scare you off. But don't worry. I don't have unrealistic—"

"Angus. Be quiet and show me the sign." Angus took a deep breath but still held the paper against him. "Please?"

He slowly turned the sign around.

"The Future Charles Barclay"

I caught my breath. "I was not expecting that."

"Sorry. Are you frea—"

I cut off his words with a kiss.

Epilogue

One Year Later

"Hey, Charlotte. You got a minute?" Margaret Atkinson, my project coordinator at Hallmark, stood just outside my create space. It was really just a slightly larger than average cubicle, but Margaret thought the word cubicle stifled our imaginative spirits, so while most of the Hallmark designers worked in cubicles, Margaret's team worked in create spaces.

"Sure."

"Let's go down to the conference center."

Margaret was a tiny woman with short legs, so I slowed my pace to match hers.

"Have you and your husband found a new place?" Margaret asked.

"We found an adorable little house in Gladstone last weekend. I think we're going to take it. It's about the same distance from the hospital, but it will make my

193

commute a lot easier."

"That sounds perfect." She sounded a little more enthusiastic than I would have expected.

I didn't recognize the two other people in the conference room, but they seemed to be expecting us. Margaret shook their hands and then turned to me. "This is Charlotte Barclay. She's the one who submitted the proposal. This is Doug Johnson and Ellery Standifer."

So this little impromptu meeting was about my proposal? I tried not to act too excited.

"Charlotte, it's good to meet you." Mr. Johnson said.

"You, too."

"I loved your proposal." It was Ms. Standifer. "What a brilliant idea. And what a great way to give back to the community."

"Tell us how you came up with the idea."

I sat forward in my chair. "A little over a year ago, my husband had a patient with a condition that required he be in traction for almost two weeks. He was only six years old, and after about a week, he was beside himself. He was depressed and angry and was acting out. It was hard for him and his parents, especially his mother, who was there with him almost all the time. At the time, I was working at Imaginarium, and Angus had the idea that maybe I could do one of the craft projects I was doing with the children at Imaginarium with this little boy. He took to it immediately and the rest of his stay was pleasant. He just needed something fun to do to take his mind off what was happening to him."

"I'm glad you submitted the proposal," Mr. Johnson said. "We'd like to launch a program that would be in conjunction with Imaginarium and we'd like you to be in charge of it."

Ms. Standifer slid an envelope across the table to me. "We'd like you to design a variety of projects that would be

194

easy to take into hospitals in the community, things that children will enjoy and can make their stay a little more interesting. Obviously what's entertaining for a small child will be boring for an older child, so you'll need to come up with a variety of projects that would be appropriate for different age groups. We'll provide the supplies and you can work with the hospitals to tailor the program for their needs."

"We'll leave it up to you to let us know if you'd like an assistant to work with you. I'd imagine that starting out, you might not need one, but if the program is successful, you'll probably need help."

I wasn't sure what to say. When I had submitted the idea, I hadn't pictured myself being the one to do it, although the thought of it did excite me.

"I'm sure you'll want to talk it over with your husband," Margaret said.

"Yes, I would."

"Can you let us know by the end of the week?" Ms. Standifer asked.

"We'd like to get started right away," Mr. Johnson added.

"Of course."

"Take that with you." She pointed at the envelope. "We want you to know exactly what we're planning to do before you take it on."

"Please tell me you don't have to work late," I said when Angus answered his phone. "I'm leaving the office right now, and I can't wait to talk to you. In person."

"What's going on?"

"I got offered a job and I want us to go over everything together and decide if I should take it."

"What job?"

"No, no, no. We're not talking about it over the phone. Just hurry home, okay?"

"I'll get there as soon as I can."

"Thank you. I love you."

"I love you, too."

It still thrilled me to be able to say those words so easily to each other. It was hard to imagine that barely a year ago we had been unsure of our future together. What a difference a year can make. Our wedding had been exactly what I had wanted. Angus had chosen Luigi's for our rehearsal dinner and had asked everyone to be our therapists for the evening, sharing good advice, funny stories, and lots of laughter. Our honeymoon was spent moving everything from our apartments into a spacious two-bedroom in the A building. A real honeymoon to somewhere romantic and wonderful would have to wait until Angus could get a little more time off.

I don't know how he managed it, but Angus almost beat me home.

"You're not going to believe this," I said.

"First things first, Charles." He pulled me into his arms and kissed me.

I put my arms around his neck and kissed him back. "What did you call me?" I said against his lips.

"Sorry, Charlotte." He emphasized my name. He called me Charlotte most of the time now, but every once in a while, he'd forget and call me one of the old nicknames. I wasn't crazy about any of them, but Charles had to go. For obvious reasons.

"That's better."

After a minute, I pried my lips away and pulled him by

the hand to the counter, where my new job offer was waiting.

"Imaginarium Outreach? What's that?"

We sat down, and I told Angus about my meeting. "They liked the idea and they want me to be in charge of implementing it."

"That's great, but you wanted to design."

"I know. I'll still be designing. They want me to come up with the art projects."

Angus grinned. "Art, huh?"

I smiled back. "Art, crafts. You know. Probably some of both."

"Uh huh." He leaned forward and kissed me just under my ear.

It was difficult to stay focused when he did that, so I pushed him away. "Anyway, they want me to design the projects and work with the hospitals to make it work for them. And I get a raise. And an assistant if all goes well."

"You know whatever you decide is fine with me. I just want you to be happy."

"I am happy." I put my hand on his cheek.

"Do you want to do this?"

I nodded. "All afternoon I've been thinking about Braxton and the change that came over him. And then I got home and saw that." I nodded toward the Christmas tree Braxton had given to Angus. It now hung on our new refrigerator. "I want to do it."

"Then you, Mrs. Barclay, have a new job. I think we should celebrate."

"Say it again," I said.

"I think we should celebrate?" he asked.

"No. The other part."

Angus pulled me into his arms. "The Mrs. Barclay part?"

I put my arms around his neck. "Yeah, that's my favorite."

He covered my mouth with his and kissed me like he meant it. "This is my favorite."

I might have agreed, but my mouth was otherwise occupied.

Author's Message

I *'m honored that you decided to spend some time with one of my books. Thank you1 Thank you! I hope you enjoyed Charlotte and Angus's story. As I wrote the series, I realized I wanted to know if Aleena and Flynn will get a happily ever after (not necessarily together). Sometime in the near future, we'll find out. Sign up for my newsletter on my website (http://kareywhite.com) for the latest updates on their stories and others. While you're there, feel free to send me a message. I love to hear from readers!*

As an author, I hope to have happy readers who spread the word about my books. If you'd be willing, I'd be so grateful for a review on Goodreads or Amazon or wherever else you might share your thoughts on books.

Happy Reading!

Karey

Acknowledgements

It always feels like such an accomplishment when I finish a book. I feel like I deserve a box of See's chocolates and a little vacation. And then I remember all the people who have helped make it happen and I know there are a whole host of people who deserve a box of chocolates.

Thank you to Dad, Mom, Veronica, Savannah, and Lori, who are my enthusiastic, cheerleading first readers. Thank you to Leslie, Rachael, Kathy, Kaylee, Missy, Corinne, and Stephanie who were beta readers on this series and offered valuable feedback.

An enormous thank you to Rachael, who deserves her own paragraph on this book. It's so great to have a friend and fellow author who is willing to jump in and help me with whatever I need. We never know when life is going to throw us several curveballs at once. This time it was an emergency room visit and a death in the family that meant a funeral in another part of the country. Rachael jumped in and formatted the entire book for me so I could attend to personal matters and still make my deadline. Thank you!

Thanks to Lori and Lisa for good treats. Thank you to Dale and Renae for making their lovely cabin my writing retreat. Thank you to Leslie, Connor, Michaela and Rachael for the beautiful cover. Thank you to all of you who read and send lovely words of encouragement.

Most of all, thanks to my family, Travis, Bruce, Veronica, Savannah and Joseph. I have the best husband and children, and I am so grateful for all you do to help me succeed.

About the Author

K arey grew up in Idaho, Oregon, Missouri and Utah. Through the years, she's been a student, a teacher, a secretary, a clothing designer and seamstress, a wedding cake maker, a crafter, a scrapbooker, a cook, a housekeeper (alright, this skill she's still working on) a homework helper (until they pass her in math, somewhere around the third grade), and a calm and ladylike fan at her children's sporting events.

Nothing makes her happier than being with family and friends, eating good food and sharing good conversation and a few laughs. When she's with witty and clever people, she could stay there for hours. She loves to travel and see new places. Someday she hopes to take research trips to Norway, Iceland, Scotland, Denmark (while the tulips are in bloom), China, and New Zealand.

She and her husband are the parents of four children that make them look good. She loves salmon and marzipan (not necessarily together) and getting letters. Find out more about Karey and her books at kareywhite.com

If you enjoyed The Husband Maker series, you'll enjoy the Meet Your Match series by Rachael Anderson.